# Other Ones

Ana Elisa Naveira

AOS Publishing, 2025



ISBN: 978-1-998662-87-6

Cover Design: Meredith Lindsay

Visit AOS Publishing's website:
www.aospublishing.com

Then solitude. Now multitude.

# Chapters

# One

The last-minute camping trip served as a pretext for Beto and Tadeu to reconnect after years of lost contact. Ever since Beto had moved to the capital for his studies, his visits to the countryside had become increasingly rare, even though it was only a two-hour drive, it had been years since he last showed up. A sense of strangeness lingered between them. It was hard to believe that these two near strangers had once grown up together, sharing a childhood full of adventures.

Life had happened, and in completely opposite ways for each of them. Now, here they were, sitting in the very spot that had once been so familiar. The place where they had made countless plans and tried to imagine what the future would hold. The place that had witnessed so much laughter, so many arguments, small fights, and quiet reconciliations. The conversation was slow to pick up; their topics diverged.

The university buzzed with students full of life, dreams, and ambitions. Beto's new job at a renowned and respected multinational company, along with friendships with people from various parts of the country and the world, had transformed him into a new person. Now accustomed to the traffic and chaos of the city, spending a weekend in the countryside had become synonymous with boredom.

Beto was a handsome guy, the type who effortlessly attracted the attention of both women and men wherever he went. With his serious demeanor, neatly tailored clothes, and impeccably slicked-back hair, he was the quintessential catch. A hard worker—perhaps too much so, his mother Ivone would complain—he had ambitions of rising high in the company. Methodical, he organized his clothes by color and style in his apartment closet. He didn't have much of a sense of humor and tended to be quiet and reserved. Even unintentionally, he exuded an air of superiority, which was his greatest flaw.

Tadeu, on the other hand, couldn't care less about how he dressed and was always sporting a scruffy beard. His brown hair had no defined style, yet he was still a handsome man in his own right, a kind of beauty he never allowed himself to show. He hid behind his careless appearance, as if it were a shield that could protect him from people in general. His goal was to go unnoticed wherever he went.

Beto ended up agreeing to meet Tadeu at his mother's insistence. Tadeu had been his neighbor throughout his life in the countryside and still lived in the same house. He practically shared the same garden with Ivone, across the narrow cobblestone street.

After Beto moved to the city, Tadeu essentially became Ivone's new son. He was a very lonely person, as his parents had passed away long ago, so he was always available to help Ivone with whatever she needed.

Tadeu hadn't been as fortunate as his childhood friend. He had grown up in a complicated family and hadn't received the support needed to pursue his dreams—neither in the form of emotional support nor money.

Their town, which had once been one of the most promising in the region, now suffered tremendous neglect after the two factories, the main sources of local employment and income, shut down. The center was filled with graffiti-covered walls, drunkards who slept on the sidewalks, and beggars persistently asking for money. The small town, even with its historic houses, old buildings, and steep hills lined with souvenir shops, was no longer as attractive to tourists as it once was. And to make matters worse, the weather didn't help keep tourism alive. The sky was always gray and rainy, and the cold, foggy nights gave the whole place a somber appearance. In the morning, the sidewalks were always wet, and the trees woke up dripping with dew.

The place Beto and Tadeu chose for camping was no mere coincidence. The trail to the old abandoned power plant had always been their favorite spot as children. As soon as they arrived, they sat by the river, just like they used to. They lit a bonfire and sipped on beer while admiring the flames pirouetting in the air. A trail of mist crept along the forest floor, enveloping stones and tree trunks along the way. The cold was biting.

With a stick, Tadeu poked at the campfire, making it crackle.

During their  time there, they had talked about almost everything - what they were currently going through, their lives, their jobs. They spoke about how they still watched sports even though they didn't play anymore, and how the world seemed to be getting worse. "These kids nowadays," they said, shaking their heads.

It felt strange to reintroduce yourself to someone who once knew everything about you. They had talked about the time they'd spent apart, and about how life had brought them new experiences in the meantime. Beto could have spent hours talking about all the trips he had taken, all the women he had met... but for some reason, he didn't feel comfortable doing so just yet.

Many old stories were also brought up — skipping class, falling for the same girl at school, playing pranks on the older folks, or driving the local shop owner crazy while trying to steal cigarettes. The kind of things kids from small towns do for fun.


That way, the initial awkwardness was starting to fade, slowly giving way to a warm sense of nostalgia. The hours, which until then had seemed to drag on, began to return to their normal pace. After much conversation, the pace of the topic started to slow down, and now they were silent, just listening to the mysterious sounds the forest emitted deep into the early morning. The glow from the campfire illuminated their faces, half in view and half in shadow. At that moment, Tadeu found it quite fitting to begin to vent.

"Beto, I know it's been a long time since we've seen each other, but I don't have anyone else to talk to anymore." His voice sounded hesitant; nevertheless, he continued, "I've been worried for some time now. Maybe I should see a doctor, a psychiatrist, I don't know."

He knew that, even if their friendship wasn't as strong as it once was, he could still say these kinds of things to someone who had known him his whole life. For some reason, that fact brought him a sense of comfort and safety.

"Did something happen?" Beto adjusted himself in the folding chair.

"A few weeks ago, I started seeing things." Tadeu paused, inhaling deeply. "At first, I thought it was just my imagination, something in my head, an optical illusion, I don't know. I would wake up in the middle of the night hearing noises, the front door opening or closing. When I rushed into the living room to see what or who it was, there was never anyone to be found. After a while, I began to notice the presence of what seemed to be a man. At first, I only saw his silhouette: a blur, a shapeless figure."

Tadeu stirred a twig on the ground and continued.

"Once, I woke up in the middle of the night and found that figure standing right beside me, at the door of my room, staring at me. I was terrified."

"Watching you? Observing you as you sleep? What do you mean?" Beto frowned, still incredulous about what he had just heard.

"Yes, all the lights in the house were off, but I usually sleep with the window open, so the room was dimly lit by the streetlight, and that's how I could see so clearly..."

"And what was it? Could you see anything?." Beto asked, curious.

"Yes. And the most frightening thing is that the man looking at me... was myself."

Beto was at a loss for how to react to that information. He couldn't hide his astonishment, so he waited for Tadeu to elaborate further.

"I can assure you, the face, the mannerisms, the hair... everything! Even the clothes... well, not exactly the same, but very similar. I rubbed my eyes to make sure it wasn't an illusion, and when I opened them again, the guy wasn't there anymore."

The two remained silent for several seconds, gazing at the fire.

Not knowing how to elaborate further on the topic, Beto asked, "And now, what are you going to do?"

"I thought about installing cameras in the house, the ones with sensors, you know? Max didn't hear anything either, and he always barks at any noise."

Beto took the last sip from the beer can, crushed it, and stuffed it into the plastic bag he had brought to collect the trash.

Tadeu seemed worried, unsure if it had been a good idea to reveal all that information, but there was no one else he could share it with. And Beto was a smart guy; surely he wouldn't try to take him to an exorcism session. It was more likely that his friend would try to find a more realistic solution.

Beto didn't know how to react to that, so he chose to remain silent, reflecting for a while. That was very typical of him. Better to say nothing than to say something foolish.

After the confession, they remained there, standing, watching the fire, and drinking beer. Away from the campfire, the cold was unbearable. The sound of water flowing in the creek cut through the silence of the night.

# Two

Beto and Tadeu woke up late the next day. The toll of saying goodbye to their youth was evident, and both of their backs were sore. The last time they had camped together, they must have been around sixteen years old. It was a day when Tadeu had argued with his father and sought refuge to avoid sleeping at home. So he had ventured into the forest with Beto, carrying a backpack full of junk food and several beers. That place had become their secret little spot.

Whenever they wanted to escape their own lives, that's where they would go. Beto and Tadeu built their friendship because they were raised together, neighbors with adjoining walls. They grew up playing in the street—staying out late playing soccer or inventing countless adventure stories, time passing by in a blur until they were suddenly being called home for dinner by their respective mothers. It was common for them to arrive home filthy after exploring every possible corner of the city, whether on foot or by bicycle.

As they grew up and became teenagers, their differences in interests began to show. Beto, more focused on his studies, didn't miss the opportunity to go away to college. With the distance, their divergent personalities couldn't sustain the relationship. But now that Beto had more time to come back on weekends, it was inevitable that they would reconnect, especially because Tadeu was so present in Ivone's life.

Tadeu didn't have the same opportunity to leave the countryside. After his parents' deaths, he had remained living alone in the house. In his loneliness, he had seized a few opportunities to make money illicitly, with people who weren't exactly good company. His so-called "friends" often used his house to store drugs and some stolen goods.

★ ★ ★ ★ ★

Ivone announced that she had invited a friend over for dinner. She had met Beatriz at church recently, a widow who had recently moved to the countryside in search of a quieter life. Beatriz was familiar with the town, as her brother had been the mayor there a few years earlier. Ivone needed to make new friends; she was getting older and increasingly lonely in that house.

At the agreed time, Beatriz rang the doorbell. She was accompanied by her daughter, Cintia, who had been reluctantly persuaded to accompany her mother amidst a barrage of arguments about how "Ivone has a son your age who also lives in the capital; you'll get along well." Cintia only agreed to go because she needed to support her mother. Besides, she would be leaving there in a few days, and would feel more at ease knowing that her mother wouldn't be feeling so lonely in her countryside life.

Beatriz had certainly been a beautiful woman in her youth; that much was clear. And even though aging was inevitable, she had been lucky not to have been marred by time. Aging while maintaining beauty is quite fortunate. Cintia had inherited her mother's features—a wide, bright smile, a straight nose full of personality, and flawless skin.

During the meal, Cintia and Beto exchanged awkward glances. Under the scrutiny of their respective mothers, they didn't know what to talk about. When Ivone finished clearing the dishes from the table and announced that dessert would be served in a few moments, Beto took the opportunity to step out onto the balcony. He felt suffocated by the situation. He couldn't stand his mother's traps, always trying to introduce him to a "nice girl".

He watched the deserted street, devoid of any movement, with just the mist hovering over the road. He heard Max barking. Tadeu's German Shepherd was sitting in the garden, looking back at Beto; they hadn't met yet. Beto took the opportunity to do something he hadn't done in a long time: he pulled out a pack of cigarettes from his pocket, lit one, and, after taking a drag, exhaled a puff of smoke. The cold and dampness turned the smoke into a thick, voluminous shape, an abstract sculpture.

He heard the front door being opened and, looking back, saw Cintia standing there awkwardly, her hands smoothing her arms as if trying to warm herself from the cold.

"Hi. Do you need anything?" Beto asked.

"No. I just came here to introduce myself properly, without our mothers' interference." She chuckled warmly. "My name is Cintia, nice to meet you." She extended her hand, her ponytail swaying from side to side.

In a lighthearted manner, they staged a small act, as if they were meeting each other for the first time. Without their mothers' watchful eyes, they felt more at ease to chat.

"I'm Beto. I heard you also live in the capital?"

"Yes. I'm a dentist there; I have a practice in the Northern area."

"That's great! I'll remember that when I have a toothache." It was the closest Beto could come to making a joke.

The house's balcony was small, with a rocking chair tucked in one corner and a waist-high wall in front of the door. A small lawn stretched out ahead, where Ivone's well-tended garden also lay. It ended at a low stone wall with a small white gate that led directly onto the sidewalk. For some reason, this area still didn't require high walls, electric fences, security cameras, or guard posts.

Beto liked the neighborhood where he had spent his childhood, playing in the streets—a place that was still safe and where everyone knew each other. He had fond memories of that place, but he preferred the traffic and chaos of the city, which he wouldn't trade for anything.

"Are you from here originally?" Beto asked Cintia. "Why don't I remember you and your mother? I lived here for almost my entire life, and practically everyone knows each other."

"We used to live in another city nearby," Cintia explained, trying to warm her hands. "After my father passed away, we moved to the capital. I graduated and started working a lot, and my mother, feeling very lonely, decided to move back to the countryside. She didn't want to return to our hometown; there were too many memories of my father there. She wanted a change of scenery and tranquility, so she came here recently. We have some relatives here, and one of my uncles was even the mayor of the city a few years ago."

"I see."

The lampposts formed small circles of light on the ground. Suddenly, Tadeu appeared in that dimly-lit scene, next to the small gate on the sidewalk. Beto signaled for him to come in.

"Come on in, buddy. My mom made pudding. By the way, this is Cintia. And this is Tadeu." He gestured to introduce each of them.

After a while, accompanied by a slice of pudding, Tadeu returned to the balcony. He wondered to himself, *Where did the girl come from?* He had found Cintia attractive.

Beto talked about his job at the multinational where he worked, describing how his role was crucial in making various company decisions. He held a good position and had his own office, complete with a beautiful desk and a nice view from the window, high up in the most imposing commercial building in the region. As if life wasn't busy enough, he openly admitted to being a workaholic. When he managed to find time, he would jog in the park to stay active. Beto believed that not only the mind but also the body should be prepared and in good shape. Moreover, he used his running time to organize his thoughts.

Tadeu watched the whole scene in silence. He didn't have anything particularly interesting to share about his life and didn't feel confident talking about his own professional activities after Beto's elaborate speech. When he occasionally had some money left over, he managed to save it in a savings account. His simple lifestyle wasn't appealing to women in general, let alone those from the big city.

He stood there fascinated, watching Cintia eagerly talk about her daily life. Tadeu realized he enjoyed admiring the smiling girl as she happily discussed her profession. She seemed like a nice person, articulate with a lively conversation. It had been a long time since Tadeu had met someone like her. Where he lived, he was surrounded by housewives or simpler folks from the small town. They talked for hours on end, unaware of the time passing by.

# Three

It was early morning when Tadeu opened his eyes and waited for his vision to adjust to the darkness. He had gone to bed late after chatting with Beto and Cintia into the wee hours. The living room TV was on, making noise—he didn't remember leaving it on. He always made sure to turn it off before leaving the house. Then again, he had had a few beers and had come home somewhat intoxicated.

He rose lazily, rubbing his eyes. The memory of the figures he had been seeing recently sent a shiver down his spine. He took a deep breath and stood up slowly, trying not to make any noise. Though he hated to admit it, he was scared. Walking on tiptoe to avoid the creaking wooden floor, he left the lights off, relying on the street lamps' glow to see. The house was small, and with a few more steps toward the door, he could see the living room.

His eyes couldn't believe what they were witnessing: there he was, lying on the living room sofa, sleeping with the remote control in his hand. The face was identical to his, as were the body, the skin, and the hair. It was so typical of Tadeu to fall asleep on the sofa that it wasn't surprising that this other Tadeu did the same. The TV was on, playing some late-night movie. The lamp above was off, and only the flickering light from the screen irregularly illuminated the room.

Tadeu stood there, frozen, watching the surreal scene. It was like being a spectator in his own life, a real-life movie too dull to be sold in cinemas. He was a spectator of himself.
Where was Max? He missed the German Shepherd, who always lay at his feet, guarding his sleep no matter where Tadeu chose to nap. Max was neither with him nor with the version of himself in the living room.

Was he dreaming? He shut his eyes tightly, scrunching his face. "Wake up, wake up!" the voice in his head screamed. When he opened his eyes, he waited a few seconds for the darkness to fade. The man was still there.

The front door of the house began to tremble, producing a hollow, yet very loud sound. He realized something was scratching the wood forcefully.

*Max is outside!* Tadeu had come home so drunk that he had left the poor dog out in the cold. Everything was so confusing. The man lying on the sofa woke up from the noise. Tadeu felt his face heat up.

Both of them could hear Max scratching at the door.

His stomach felt like ice, and his hands were tingling.

He waited in silence.

The other man got up, sighed, and slowly walked to the door without turning on the light, appearing dazed. Max ran into the room. Outside, a light rain was falling, and the dog was wet. The man had also heard the noise at the door but seemed not to notice Max, deliberately ignoring him. This only made the situation even stranger.

Max nestled into his favorite corner of the sofa and stayed there, gazing at the strange man standing in the dim light. Then he looked around for Tadeu, but didn't find him, sensing that the other man, though very similar, was not his owner. Tadeu had already gone back to the bedroom.

Tadeu heard the television being turned off and footsteps approaching the room where he was. Unsure of what to do, he slipped under the bed, intending to wait until the man fell asleep before finding the right moment to come out.

The man collapsed heavily onto the mattress, took a deep breath, adjusted a bit, and eventually fell asleep. Within moments, he began to snore. Tadeu started to move carefully, not wanting to wake the man sleeping above his head, or Max. He crossed the room silently,

reached the front door, and turned the handle very slowly. His heart was pounding wildly; miraculously, the dog didn't hear a thing.
Confused and unsure of what to do, Tadeu headed to Beto's house. He called his friend's cell phone so as not to ring the doorbell and startle Ivone at that late hour. Beto answered with a sleepy voice and quietly came downstairs to open the door.
"It happened again, Beto. He's there, he's in my house, sleeping in my bed!" Tadeu gestured, distressed.
"What? How so? Who's he?" Beto was still half asleep.
"The man I told you about, the man who looks just like me!"

They both rushed to Tadeu's house, crossing the garden illuminated only by the moonlight. They opened the door and turned on the light as they entered the bedroom. Max straightened up on the sofa, lifting his head in alert.
No one was there.
"Beto, am I going crazy? I saw the guy napping in the living room with the TV on. He woke up and then went to the bedroom. I hid under the bed, waited for him to fall asleep, and came out," Tadeu said in a trembling voice.
"Relax, it's okay. I think it's best if you stay at my place tonight."
"Only if Max can come with me."
"Of course."

# Four

The next morning, they gathered around the table with Ivone for breakfast. She was delighted to have her son's company, uncertain of when she would see him again. She was also pleased to see Tadeu reconnect with Beto. With a smile, she served coffee, milk, French bread, butter, cream cheese, and a simple homemade cake.

After the meal, the two young men said their goodbyes and returned to Tadeu's house. Some shy rays of sunshine tried to pierce through the clouds, but the chilly wind still sent shivers down their spines. The cobblestone street was deserted, with only Odete, an elderly neighbor, sweeping her sidewalk a few meters away.

Back at Tadeu's home, everything remained as it was—nothing overturned or disturbed, no signs of anyone having slept there. Tadeu suggested to Beto that they look for a security equipment store. Determined to install cameras in his house, he knew of a place downtown where they might find something suitable. They headed there together.

* * * * *

As with most small towns in the region, this one had a central square where the mayor held local events. At its center stood a bandstand where the church's youth band rehearsed on Sundays. The fountain, for some unknown reason, had been deactivated for a few months. At this time of morning, elderly people could be seen playing chess or checkers at the concrete tables. The popcorn vendor had his cart set up, though business was still slow. Most shops had opened, awaiting customers. In better times, tourists would have been bustling through the center, seeking a peaceful weekend away from their busy lives. However, lately, such interest had waned as the region showed signs of decline. Hotels struggled with a lack of guests, and more and more restaurants and cafés were going out of business.

Tadeu and Beto walked along the narrow sidewalk until they found a shop that likely had the items they were looking for. Amid various household utensils and technological knick-knacks, they hoped to find security cameras. As they entered, a bell above the door chimed, and moments later, a mustached man in a tight-fitting polo shirt appeared. They explained that they needed a camera that recorded well at night.

The man pointed to a shelf displaying various devices, such as digital cameras, webcams, and, lower down, several security camera kits. After evaluating the options, they decided on a kit with two cameras that not only stored footage on a server but also allowed real-time access to the images via mobile phone. The shop owner noted that he wasn't accustomed to selling such products to local residents, as the town was relatively safe and many people didn't even lock their doors. It was more common for stores, businesses, and factories to install security equipment. Nevertheless, it was good to offer these products to individuals, as occasionally, residents from neighboring towns sought similar equipment.

Beto and Tadeu decided to install the equipment themselves, knowing it would be difficult to find someone in town to do it for them. In such a small town, everything was challenging.

On their way to Tadeu's house, they spotted a familiar face in the small crowd gathered on the sidewalk: Cintia.

"Hey! What are you guys doing downtown?" Cintia greeted them.

"Not much. Tadeu came to buy some cameras to see if... if he can catch the kids who've been playing pranks at his house at night," Beto improvised.

"Are such things really happening here? I thought the town was peaceful," Cintia remarked, sounding surprised.

"Well, it didn't used to happen, but lately it's been occurring. I think it's harmless. What about you? What brings you here today?" Beto quickly changed the subject.

"I came to buy some things my mom asked for, like sewing thread and fabric. Are you guys doing anything later?" She brushed a strand of hair away from her face and tucked it behind her ear.

"We don't have any plans... Do you want to do something?"

"Hm, I don't think there are many options around here, right? But maybe I'll text you later?"

"Sure."

Back at Tadeu's house, the guys spent the rest of the morning installing and testing the cameras, all under the watchful gaze of Max, who didn't understand what was going on but displayed his canine curiosity. Once they successfully completed the job, they were quite satisfied with the outcome. Now they had the means to gather evidence that Tadeu wasn't losing his mind.

They had lunch with Ivone, who had prepared a wonderful roast beef with rice, beans, and potatoes. As always, the salad was solemnly ignored. The juice was made from guavas picked directly from the backyard guava tree. That was one of the advantages of small-town life: everything was practical and simple. Homemade food, prepared with maternal care, certainly had a special taste. However, after lunch, Beto and Tadeu faced a rather monotonous day ahead, with nothing else to do.

Small towns do have their share of boring moments.

# Five

In the late afternoon, Cintia sent a message to Beto's phone:
*"What are you up to?"*
They exchanged a few messages and agreed to meet at a bar near the main square downtown. Cintia enjoyed spending time with her mother in the countryside but often missed having more friends and commitments. That's why she saw Beto and Tadeu as potential companions. Since Beto also lived in the capital, the idea of deepening their new friendship seemed promising.
Cintia was a great girl, the kind any guy would want to date. She was fun-loving and cheerful. Very focused on her career, she loved what she did—always staying updated, frequently attending courses, and treating her first and last patients of the day with the same enthusiasm. But this level of dedication left little time for friendships. As a result, she didn't have many close friends, and it was rare for her to go out for fun—to a bar, a club, or anything like that. Despite living in a large and cosmopolitan city, she didn't seize all the opportunities available and ended up spending many weekends at home. She devoted herself to taking care of her cats. She adored her pets and had two, even in her small apartment. Her mother often insisted she needed a new boyfriend—Cintia had been single for some time now.
Her last relationship had been quite promising and long, but one day she discovered she was being cheated on—her boyfriend had been involved with a coworker. To make matters worse, Cintia found out the other woman was pregnant. Since then, she had found it very difficult to fully trust anyone. In fact, the trauma was much deeper than she let on. Cintia liked to show that everything was always okay, despite her inner struggles.
They sat at the iron table on the sidewalk and ordered bottled beers. The sun had already disappeared behind the gray clouds. As their lively conversation continued, a stout man entered the bar and, on

his way out, greeted Tadeu, who responded reluctantly. He was one of his father's old friends—or rather, one of the acquaintances his father had made over the years at the bar.

The chubby man wore a short-sleeved button-down shirt, with nearly all the buttons undone, revealing a significant portion of his round belly overlapping his waistband. Despite the cold weather, he wasn't wearing a coat; in fact, he looked sweaty and greasy. Around his neck hung a gold chain with a shiny crucifix that caught everyone's eye. He was clearly rough and uncouth in appearance. It was evident he was drunk, as confirmed when he opened his mouth:

"Tadeu, Tadeu... are you turning into your father, Walmir?" He burst into loud, mocking laughter.

Embarrassed, Tadeu didn't respond; he simply returned the taunting with an awkward smile and looked away. He didn't want Cintia to hear such comments; he was trying hard to make a good impression.

"Booze is a cage, man!" insisted the unpleasant drunkard, kissing his fingertips in an exaggerated manner.

Alcohol was Walmir's second greatest passion—second only because his first love was his wife, Arlete. Walmir had been deeply in love and suffered a great disillusionment shortly after Tadeu was born, when Arlete unexpectedly abandoned her son and husband to wander the world. No one ever uncovered her motivations.

It was then that Márcia, a very close cousin of Arlete, offered to help take care of the baby. Over time, Márcia and Walmir grew so close that they ended up getting married. However, rumor had it that Walmir was never able to forget his ex-wife, the great love of his life. Tadeu thought, *Man, what an annoying guy*, as he stood up and approached the fat man, staring him directly in the eyes.

"Could you please excuse us, sir?" he raised his voice.

"Alright, alright... I was just kidding," the man responded awkwardly.

The drunkard, speaking slurred and blinking slowly, raised his hands with palms exposed in a gesture of surrender, somewhat pushing Tadeu away while signaling an end to the dispute. Tadeu returned to the table, facing the questioning gazes of his friends. Beto knew very well the reasons behind that embarrassing situation. Over the years, Walmir had unfortunately transformed into a different person. He used to be a very simple, hardworking, and honest man. However, with time, he found himself lost to alcohol, often staying out late in bars, where he encountered the kind of people Tadeu had just dealt with.

It didn't take long before Walmir started to mistreat Márcia. Initially, the abuse was verbal, but over the years, it escalated to physical violence. By the end of his life, people said Walmir had gone mad. It was common to see him talking to himself in front of the house, but he never made much sense.

Tadeu held a deep affection for Márcia. When she passed away, she left him all the money she had saved throughout her life. Márcia had embraced the idea of raising Tadeu and made it her sole source of joy. Tadeu was incredibly grateful to her; he had never felt the absence of his biological mother, whom he rarely asked about. He had never been interested in knowing her whereabouts or taken steps to find her.

* * * * *

The night fell, bringing with it a cold temperature. By this time, Tadeu, Beto, and Cintia were huddled together, rubbing their hands to keep warm. It was a sign that it was time to head back home. Surely, Ivone would soon call to inquire about her son's whereabouts. "What mischief are you up to in this town? You always complained there was nothing to do here!"

# Six

Tadeu crossed the small gate to his house, leaving it ajar as usual. Max came running toward him, licking his face and seeking affection. During the day, Tadeu sometimes let Max roam the yard, but at bedtime, he always brought the dog inside. As he reached the porch, he fumbled for his keys in his pocket; the light was off, and he couldn't see well. He was startled when he heard voices coming from inside.

He pressed his ear to the door, trying to understand what was happening. He heard a voice very similar to his own, but couldn't make out the words. There was also a feminine voice. *Who could it be? What are they talking about?*

He signaled for Max to be quiet and motioned for the dog to sit, hoping the animal would understand. His breathing quickened, his nerves on edge. He turned the doorknob as quietly as possible and opened the door slowly; the people inside the house kept talking. He entered the room and stood in front of the slightly open door, unable to believe what he was witnessing.

Seated on the couch, Cintia was commenting on a news piece on TV. It was about a group of young people who had been robbed in the capital; one of them had been held hostage for hours.

"It's this kind of thing I don't miss about the capital. Life in the countryside is much more peaceful, without these violent crimes," she said. She sat cross-legged on the couch, wearing an outfit very similar to the one she had been wearing earlier at the bar. Tadeu couldn't recall all the details, but he remembered the blue knitted sweater and jeans. Her boots were strewn across the floor. She was now only wearing socks.

He heard a male voice respond from the kitchen.

"True, I like living here. When I need to, I'll go to a bigger city nearby, but generally, I have everything I need right here."

It was exactly the response Tadeu would have given, to the point where he almost mouthed the words in unison with his other self, emphasizing the same phrases.

Could they not see Tadeu standing there, just in front of the door, only a few meters away? Impossible. He glanced around the room and noticed some things were different: the TV was a more modern model, one of those plasma screens, and the furniture arrangement had changed slightly. However, the couch was still the same; Tadeu had recently bought it from a friend's furniture store.

Suddenly, the man from the kitchen appeared in the living room, carrying two beers. Tadeu froze: he saw himself entering the room, like a perfect reflection in a mirror, but alive. It was another Tadeu— a flawless copy of himself. The other Tadeu opened a can and offered the second one to Cintia, who promptly accepted it.

At that moment, Tadeu felt like a ghost in his own home. He was watching everything unfold, unseen by anyone.

Max, tired of waiting on the porch, had nudged his way through the slightly open door. He sat in the middle of the living room, wagging his tail.

"Come here, Max! Get out of there!" Tadeu blurted out involuntarily.

Max hesitated, his ears twitching nervously. He looked at the couple in the room, confused about who they were, then back at Tadeu, who was now sure he wasn't the only one observing this scene.

Tadeu reached behind him and began to feel for the door, while keeping his eyes locked on the people inside. When he found the door, he took a few steps back and returned to the porch.

Max got up and ran after him. In his excitement, he clumsily bumped into the door, which slammed shut with the impact. At that moment, Tadeu noticed that the voices inside the house had stopped.

Silence.

Tadeu wasn't sure if the people had vanished or if they'd heard the door slam and were now alarmed. He crossed the lawn toward the small gate and hid behind the low wall, facing the street. He called Max, but the dog didn't follow, choosing instead to stay on the porch. A few seconds later, the door was flung open, and there stood the other Tadeu, peering outside with a concerned frown, searching for the source of the noise. He strained his eyes, scanning the surroundings, but saw no one. He didn't even notice Max standing right next to him on the porch, though the dog was staring directly at him, trying to figure out who he was. But the other Tadeu, finding nothing, gave up and went back inside.

# Seven

Feeling safe from danger, Tadeu stood up and looked around, hoping the people inside the house hadn't witnessed what had just happened. He waved to Max, signaling for the dog to come closer. Still somewhat disoriented, he noticed Odete—the oldest neighbor on the street—watching him through her window. Her serious face behind the glass, illuminated only by the streetlight, made her look like a haunting figure in an Impressionist painting.

He waved, trying to appear nonchalant, but she didn't return the greeting. She simply lowered the brown fabric curtain and vanished into the darkness.

Tadeu then opened the app for his home security cameras, hoping to see in real-time what was happening inside the house. At that exact moment, there was no one there. His fingers, slightly trembling, navigated the controls to rewind the footage back a few minutes. He pressed 'play', his mind racing.

One camera was on the porch, and the other in the living room. Through the screen of his phone, Tadeu saw himself arriving home minutes earlier, opening the door. The quality of security camera footage, especially in low light, was far from ideal, but he could make out the entire scene.

When he switched to the camera angle inside the living room, he continued to see himself alone, standing there nervously, as if watching a tennis match in the dark. In his memory, the lights had already been on when he arrived—there had been no need to turn them on. But on the small screen in his hand, there he stood, in the middle of the room, surrounded by complete darkness.

Minutes later, Max appeared, entering the room.

And the entire scene unfolded, with only Tadeu and Max as its protagonists.

No one else.

# Eight

Even if he wanted to seek out a therapist, Tadeu would have trouble finding a professional in his town. The few available were so old-fashioned that they would probably send him to church or a mental institution.

At times like these, he understood why Beto preferred the capital. There, he'd have access to a wider range of treatments and more people to talk to about what he was going through. In rural areas, everything was often simplified as "madness" or "demonic". This was precisely why Tadeu felt comfortable confiding in Beto. Since moving to the big city, his friend had become more open-minded. On the other hand, the big city had also changed Beto, turning him into a snobbish workaholic. How long had it been since Beto last visited the countryside? His mother had practically begged him to come. How many Christmases had Ivone spent alone, eating at the living room table without anyone's company? And Tadeu, too, sat alone at home, just a few meters away. They were two lonely souls that no one seemed to care about.

Tadeu had never fit in with the crowd he hung around. His friends were from wealthy families, idle young men with no ambitions, who only wanted to enjoy life. They smoked, drank, came home at dawn, and burned through their parents' money recklessly. Tadeu enjoyed partying, of course, but the money he earned from petty crimes wasn't enough to keep up with the frenetic lifestyle of the rich farmers' sons.

That became especially clear when he got into trouble with the police. His so-called friends vanished, pretending not to know him when they passed on the street. After all, heirs to traditional families couldn't be seen greeting someone with a criminal record; they had reputations to maintain, even if they weren't model citizens themselves. One day, they'd be the ones gracing the society pages of the Sunday newspapers.

The truth was, Tadeu often felt very alone.

Why did his father have to be such a rude drunk?

Why did his stepmother, the best person he'd ever known, have to die so young?

Why did his childhood best friend succeed in life, while he did not? Max was his only reliable companion, the only one who seemed to truly care. Christmas was approaching, and after New Year's, Beto would leave again. Probably Cintia, too. And once again, Tadeu would be alone. Just him and Max.

As usual.

*****

Beto and Tadeu bought snacks and beer, picking a random movie on TV to pass the time. They were spending the night at Tadeu's house. Outside, heavy rain lashed against the windows.

Inevitably, the conversation turned to Cintia. It was only a matter of time. A beautiful and friendly girl like her wouldn't go unnoticed.

"So, Beto, when are you going to make a move on her?" Tadeu asked, tossing a peanut into the air and trying to catch it in his mouth.

"What do you mean, man? Don't be ridiculous."

"Come on, you can tell she likes you," he teased, hoping to spark his friend's interest.

"She's nice, for sure, but she's not really my type. I'm focused on my career, and I don't want to waste time with women right now."

Beto never talked about his own life unless asked. He wasn't one to open up or vent. He hadn't always been this way, but the big city had made him like this. Tadeu could tell Beto had no real interest in his life anymore; he was only here because he needed something to fill the time and endure the torture of visiting the countryside.

They had finally gone quiet, just enjoying each other's company with the TV murmuring softly in the background. Gradually,

Tadeu's eyes grew heavy with sleep; the beer was taking effect. Each blink lasted longer than the last, and for brief moments, he lost awareness. The sound of the TV faded, and he even swore he was dreaming during those fleeting dozes. He eventually dozed off for a few minutes, then woke up with a start. The room looked different—just like the strange room he had seen the other night. But this time, Beto was with him, witnessing it all.

Tadeu quickly got up from the couch. He recognized the place and instinctively searched for the people who had been there before. He checked the kitchen: no one. The bathroom: empty. The room where he had slept as a child: vacant.

He opened the door to his current bedroom and found someone sleeping in his bed.

Bingo! It was him! The other Tadeu!

Tadeu poked Beto, trying to wake him, and as soon as he opened his eyes, Tadeu put a finger to his lips, signaling for silence, then gestured for Beto to come closer. Still confused, Beto complied. He stepped up to the doorway, peering into the room and scanning the bed." He saw no one.

"What? Where?" His eyes widened in confusion.

"Can't you see? Right there! There!" Tadeu pointed into the room, frantic. He was certain of what he was seeing. He was certain of what was happening.

Beto saw nothing but the disheveled bed, its blue sheets crumpled in the dim light. Tadeu insisted there was a man—himself—sleeping there, but Beto saw absolutely nothing. He didn't know if it was a joke or if he should laugh or stay serious. Unsure, he decided to play along.

The two of them checked the security camera footage on their phones. As expected, there was no one else in the room.

# Nine

It was Christmas night. Ivone had prepared the traditional turkey, white rice with raisins, and chestnut stuffing. She had bought the best wine she could find. Joining her for dinner were Cintia, Beatriz, Tadeu, and, of course, Max. They had a pleasant evening, talking and eating until they couldn't eat another bite. Cintia had taken charge of dessert, making a chocolate trifle—a convenient way for Ivone to test whether her potential future daughter-in-law could cook. The cold outside was biting; there wasn't a soul on the street, and even the beggars had found shelter.

Later, Cintia left to drop her mother off at home. After saying their goodbyes, she decided to return to Beto's house. At last, she had someone her age to spend time with. Tadeu, meanwhile, realized he was slowly becoming the third wheel as the night wore on. It was obvious Cintia was flirting with Beto, though he didn't seem to reciprocate in the way she hoped.

Yet, who could say what Cintia's real intentions were? Maybe she only wanted a brief fling with Beto, without any commitment. Women from the city weren't as fixated on marriage as those from the countryside. They didn't think about having children at Twenty, preferring to focus on their careers and often opting out of starting families altogether.

After several glasses of wine, Tadeu knew it was time to bow out gracefully and leave the two alone. He returned home with Max and idly scrolled through his phone. The dog slept on the rug nearby. Once again, Tadeu found himself alone on Christmas night—a feeling he had grown to loathe. This loneliness was probably what was driving him mad, making him see things.

Determined to approach the situation rationally, Tadeu resolved to figure out what was happening inside his head. Could the drugs he used as a teen still be affecting him? No, that didn't seem logical. It had to be his imagination. Stress could do that to people; Tadeu had heard similar stories on the news.

Between Christmas and New Year's, Tadeu began to notice a pattern in his hallucinations. They mostly occurred at night, and he almost always saw himself alone—except for that one time when Cintia was around, probably because no one else would come to visit. Sometimes he was talking on the phone with someone; other times, he'd just be there doing house chores. What was most unsettling was that the other Tadeu—the one he hallucinated—seemed to be complaining about things being moved around, items the real Tadeu had touched only minutes before.

* * * * *

On New Year's Eve, the mayor hosted a small celebration in the main square, and practically the entire town turned out. There were food stalls, fireworks, a space for children to play, and dozens of vendors selling all kinds of trinkets. Despite the cold, Cintia looked stunning in a short dress, paired with thick tights. Seeing her holding hands with Beto, Tadeu felt a twinge of jealousy. He knew Beto didn't want anything serious with her, and that their brief romance wouldn't last once he returned to the capital.

But Tadeu had no reason to worry. Cintia was smart and knew how to handle men like Beto. Besides, he had no right to expect anything different from his friend. He himself wasn't known for treating women chivalrously, so why should Beto be any different? On the first working day of the new year, Beto boarded a bus back to the capital, promising his mother that he would return as soon as possible. But everyone knew that wasn't exactly true—especially since he was only two hours away.

# Ten

For the first time in many days, the sun shone brightly, spreading warmth and allowing people to leave their coats at home. Tadeu played with Max in front of the house, tossing an orange frisbee and waiting for the dog to bring it back. Max loved the game, endlessly chasing the disc without tiring. As Tadeu watched Max, he noticed the lawn was covered with dry leaves and in desperate need of attention—it was easily the messiest and most neglected lawn on the street.

The other homes, always immaculate, belonged mostly to elderly ladies who had lived there for their entire lives. Many were widows, and others, like Ivone, lived alone because their children had gone to pursue life elsewhere. The cobblestone street was narrow, but the wide sidewalks made the neighborhood charming and peaceful, even though the rest of the city had fallen into decline due to the current mayor's poor management. Still, it remained a safe area.

Feeling a rare burst of motivation, Tadeu decided to clean the lawn. It was Saturday afternoon, his day off from work. He grabbed a roll of large black garbage bags and a rake. He swept all the leaves into a corner, careful to keep Max from scattering them. After filling the last bags and setting them by the stone wall, he went inside.

The other Tadeu was there.

The visits from the other Tadeu had become frequent, happening almost daily. Tadeu was nearly used to it. Most of the time, the other Tadeu didn't seem to notice him, but Tadeu always made sure to stay out of sight, just in case.

From his hidden spot, Tadeu observed the other Tadeu walking around the room, typing on his phone, apparently making a call.

"Hi, Cintia. How are you? ... Oh, nice. I'm calling to ask when you're coming over again. Are you busy with work? ... Oh, I see. The patients, right."

Tadeu watched, growing uneasy. The other Tadeu was talking to Cintia with a tone that suggested he had ulterior motives—the same feeling he'd had when he saw them together, drinking beers on the couch. This was odd. Cintia had been with Beto just a few days ago, and now this?

The conversation continued, and the other Tadeu arranged for Cintia to visit him the following weekend. She was busy with work—early January was always hectic for her—but she promised she'd come by car soon.

Tadeu's stomach churned. This other Tadeu was not like him. Sure, Tadeu had his flaws—he could be lazy, irresponsible, even a bit of a rogue—but he had never betrayed a friend's trust. When the police found drugs in his house, he could have ratted out several people, including the mayor's son, one of his regular clients. The case would have caused a huge scandal, but Tadeu had stayed silent. Despite everything, he had a code, a sense of honor, even if it came with resentment. He faced the consequences alone, knowing that in his line of work, loyalty was a rare thing.

The other Tadeu finished the call and left the house, leaving the door slightly ajar. Tadeu, keeping a safe distance, watched as the other Tadeu disappeared. He couldn't see him in the garden—he had the impression that the other Tadeu only existed within the walls of the house.


Moments later, the other Tadeu returned, this time with the garbage bags from the garden. Tadeu looked outside, and sure enough, the bags he had left were still there. The other Tadeu had also been cleaning the lawn, just as he had, though the phone call to Cintia was the only difference.

And then it hit Tadeu, a realization so sharp it caused a brief, piercing pain in his head.

The other Tadeu was living his own life, independently of the real Tadeu's. They were in sync, performing similar tasks, even sharing the same mundane chores like cleaning the garden. The visions always seemed to happen when Tadeu was home, especially at night, when he had more time to reflect. It made sense now.

His fear morphed into curiosity, adrenaline coursing through him. He had to know more about the other Tadeu—about his life, his choices, and most importantly, his relationship with Cintia. This other version of himself had somehow formed a connection with her that Tadeu hadn't managed to establish. What was going on between them? What had the other Tadeu done that he hadn't? After living through the monotony of a quiet, uneventful life, these visions offered Tadeu a new way to pass the time. Strange as it was, it had become his latest obsession.

# Eleven

On the following Saturday, the other Tadeu received a visit from the other Cintia. She arrived as smiley as ever, carrying a small bag to stay the weekend. It was only a two-hour drive between the town and the capital. They settled into the living room, lounging on the couch with a huge bowl of popcorn, watching a movie. The scene was unmistakably that of a couple enjoying each other's company, something Tadeu had never imagined.

Tadeu, watching from his unseen vantage point, had become more than just a casual observer—he was now deeply engrossed in the life of the other Tadeu. As time went on, these visions grew more vivid and lasted longer. What started as brief glimpses had evolved into full-fledged experiences, immersing him in the other Tadeu's world. It was an escape from his own dull life, and each day it became harder to pull himself away.

This alternate life was much more appealing, especially because Cintia was part of it. Even though she wasn't technically "his" Cintia, Tadeu found himself increasingly infatuated with her. He was more than physically attracted to her—he was falling in love. Seeing the other Tadeu with her filled him with a strange kind of joy. He dreamed about being in that life, about living those moments.

* * * * *

Back in his own life, Tadeu struggled to concentrate at work. He began withdrawing from social interactions, even missing dinners at Ivone's house. Beto's mother, noticing the change, grew concerned. She feared that Tadeu might be slipping back into bad habits—the same crowd that once got him involved in drug dealing. She called Beto, asking him to check on his friend. Beto dismissed her concerns, insisting that Tadeu was an adult and could manage on his own.

Still, Beto's conscience nudged him, and he texted Tadeu:

"What about those visions? Still happening?"

"No, it's all good. They've decreased a lot," Tadeu replied, lying through his teeth. This was his secret now, and he wasn't about to share it with anyone. It had become his private hobby, a hidden obsession.

Tadeu took the opportunity to ask about Cintia:

"And how's everything going with Cintia?"

"We've been seeing each other occasionally," Beto replied. "I've been busy with work, but she mentioned that she's planning to come visit soon."

Tadeu knew what would happen next: Beto would keep Cintia around for as long as she was interesting, then gradually fade from her life. Beto wasn't truly invested in her, but Tadeu was. He felt a deep connection, and though he knew he couldn't compete with someone like Beto—handsome, successful, living in the capital—he couldn't help but feel heartache.

* * * * *

Meanwhile, the relationship between the other Tadeu and the other Cintia was growing more serious. She visited almost every weekend. But something about her behavior was off. Cintia, normally so radiant and outgoing, seemed shy and withdrawn when she was with the other Tadeu. Tadeu noticed the difference, and it made him question her feelings. Was she really in love with the other Tadeu, or was there something else going on?

Jealousy began to gnaw at Tadeu—jealousy of a relationship he wasn't even part of, yet was so deeply invested in.

* * * * *

One Sunday morning, the other Cintia woke up early, leaving the other Tadeu asleep. She put on her running gear, plugged in her headphones, and went for a jog. It was a chilly morning, the sky still dark blue from the early hour. The streets were damp from the rain the night before, and the cool air filled her lungs as she ran.

Tadeu, sitting at the kitchen table, sipping coffee, heard the living room door open as she returned from her run. His heart raced at the thought of seeing her. She walked into the kitchen, sweaty and flushed, and opened the fridge to grab water. To his shock, she looked right at him.

"Awake already? So early?" she asked, smiling as she held a water bottle.

Tadeu froze. *She was talking to him.* How was this possible? He wasn't supposed to be seen. In his shock, he knocked over his coffee, spilling it across the table. Frantic, he grabbed a dishcloth to clean up the mess, but his mind was spinning.

"Tadeu, are you okay?" she asked, concerned.

Unable to process what was happening, Tadeu bolted from the kitchen and locked himself in the bathroom. His heart pounded, and his breathing became shallow. He splashed cold water on his face, staring into the mirror, trying to make sense of the situation.

From the kitchen, he could hear Cintia's voice calling for him: "Tadeu, where are you? Are you okay?"

Suddenly, he heard the other Tadeu waking up in the bedroom.

"Me? I'm here... Did you finish your run? What time is it?"

Cintia, now thoroughly confused, watched as the other Tadeu entered the kitchen, still in his pajamas, rubbing his eyes.

"Tadeu, were you sleeping? But... you were just here..."

"Me? Here? No, I was in bed," the other Tadeu replied, looking puzzled.

Cintia, clearly shaken, stood in disbelief. She had seen Tadeu in the kitchen, had spoken to him. And now, here he was again, as if nothing had happened.

"It's not possible," she whispered, trembling. The other Tadeu, seeing her distress, hugged her tightly, trying to comfort her, though he had no idea what was going on.

"Tell me, what happened?"

# Twelve

Silence.

The house was quiet. Tadeu finally emerged from the bathroom. Unsure when his "visitors" might reappear, he decided to seize the opportunity, put on a coat, and go out for a while, calling Max to join him.

He knocked on Ivone's door, and she appeared quickly.

"To what do I owe this early visit?" she asked, gesturing for him to come in as she wiped her hands on her apron.

Max, excited, dashed past them into the living room, sniffing the furniture before finding a corner to lie down, wagging his tail and observing everything attentively.

"I... I couldn't sleep," Tadeu said. "I came to see how you're doing. It's been a while since we talked."

They chatted about trivial matters. In passing, Ivone mentioned that Beto would be visiting soon and bringing Cintia with him.

"Are they dating? Is it serious?" Tadeu asked, surprised that the relationship was still going strong.

"I don't know. You young people nowadays don't seem to want anything serious with anyone. He just told me they're 'seeing each other', whatever that means."

Tadeu chuckled at her choice of words. "Well, people these days like to take a 'test drive' before starting a serious relationship, right? Besides, it's much easier to break up or get divorced nowadays. If they were around today, I would tell my stepmother to leave my father, for example."

Ivone, surprised, raised an eyebrow. "Oh, really? But... why bring that up all of a sudden?"

"I've just been thinking a lot about life lately. When we care about someone, we want to see them well, don't we? I still don't understand why my father used to hit her when he drank. The right thing would've been for him not to drink."

"It's complicated, Tadeu. At first, they were happy, like any newlywed couple. I still don't know what happened."

"Were they happy?" Tadeu asked, trying to remember. He had been very young when they married, and his memories of that time were unclear.

"Yes, they were. When your father moved next door with you, just a baby in his arms, he was lost, still grieving your mother's disappearance. At first, Márcia only came by to help. She would watch you while your father was at work. She and I talked a lot back then. She said he'd come home exhausted but still had the energy to play with you. He was a good father, though he wasn't much for household chores, like most men."

After Beto was born, Márcia and Tadeu's father grew closer. But one afternoon, Márcia showed up at Ivone's house with a black eye. When Ivone asked about it, she lied, claiming she had been hit by a falling mug while searching for something in the kitchen. Ivone didn't press her; it wasn't her style to pry. If Márcia ever wanted to talk, Ivone would be there to listen.

Tadeu had never heard these stories about his parents. His memories were mostly of arguments and his father, Walmir, being rude and leaving the house to drink with friends. Walmir had spent very little time at home, seeming to avoid his wife and son. This rejection shaped Tadeu's childhood, leaving him with a longing for a father who never seemed to want his friendship.

Talking with Ivone helped distract him from the strange events at his own house. He enjoyed her company and didn't understand why Beto avoided her so much.

As Ivone poured another cup of coffee—she liked to mix it with milk so it wouldn't be too strong—Tadeu suddenly asked, "Why do you think my father started hitting my stepmother?"

Ivone paused. "I don't know, Tadeu. From what little I heard from your stepmother, your father started spending more time away from home, didn't he? After work, instead of coming home, he'd go to the bar and stay there until late. He'd come back drunk and demand dinner... and if it wasn't ready, he'd get very angry. The next day, when he sobered up, he'd cry and apologize, begging for forgiveness."

Tadeu nodded, wanting to continue the conversation—anything to delay going back home.

"Some people say he went mad," he muttered.

"The drinking drove him mad!" Ivone agreed. "Only a crazy man would hurt someone as kind and gentle as Márcia."

Suddenly, the doorbell rang. It was Odete, the neighbor who had seen Tadeu running out of the house and hiding behind the low wall. Every Sunday morning, she stopped by Ivone's house to invite her to church. Sometimes Ivone went, sometimes she didn't.

Odete was divorced and lonely, an elderly woman who was deeply religious. Her main pastimes were attending church, flattering the priest, helping with events, and singing in the choir. Every year, she organized the town's biggest event: the barbecue and bingo, with prizes ranging from blenders to TVs and washing machines. Childless and without pets, Odete wasn't particularly warm and would probably die alone, with no one to leave her inheritance to.

"Aren't you coming to the congregation today, Ivone?" Odete asked, adjusting her dress and clearing her throat.

"Not today, Odete. Tadeu's here, so I'll keep him company."

"Tadeu should come with us. He needs it," Odete remarked, her tone brisk.

Ivone smiled politely, gripping the door as though to close it, gently ushering Odete away.

"I'll pray for both of you," Odete called, walking off.

"We appreciate it. See you later, Odete," Ivone said, closing the door.

Tadeu scratched his neck, puzzled. "Why are you friends with her?" he asked.

Through the window, they watched the old woman climb the hill towards the church, umbrella in hand, as the weather grew eerie.

# Thirteen

Beto arrived accompanied by Cintia; they had come together by car. It was far more practical to drive than to face the decrepit intercity bus. The plan was to stay only for the weekend, and it was Cintia who had insisted that Beto travel with her, as she disliked driving alone. Ivone was delighted to see that he had agreed to the girl's request, hoping that if they really were dating, Cintia would bring him closer to the family again. Beto was not the kind of guy who was very attached to family, and his tendency to prioritize work only made things worse. Ivone had always tried to keep him close; she already felt lonely, especially since Beto's father hadn't been around when he was born. Still, Beto would undoubtedly set boundaries— he wasn't going to visit the countryside every weekend, as his mother had hoped.

Cintia dropped him off at his mother's doorstep, maneuvered the car, and headed towards Beatriz's house. Ivone greeted him with a long hug.

Tadeu was sitting on the porch with Max. He was not accustomed to being there, especially with the cold weather. Beto saw him, crossed the garden, and sat next to him.

"What are you doing out here in this cold?" Beto zipped up his coat to his neck.

"Oh, nothing much... Just wanted some fresh air and to keep Max company."

"I'm here with Cintia. Want to do something later?"

"Yeah, let's do that. Just text me or give me a call."

Beto found Tadeu to be quite aloof. The last time he was in town, they had camped, talked about their lives, and spent a lot of time together. He knew he had not paid enough attention to Tadeu's hallucinations, but what could he do? He had already helped him buy and install the cameras... There was nothing more to be done about it. He did not suffer from the hallucinations his friend experienced; he had never seen anyone sleeping in his bed. He suspected that Tadeu's coldness was related to Cintia. Ever since they had both met her, Tadeu had grown more distant. Beto had hoped they might become close again, but he could sense that something was off. At first, he thought Tadeu was simply trying to give the couple some space, but eventually, he began to suspect that Tadeu might also be developing feelings for her.

It wasn't his fault that Cintia had chosen him. She had indeed chosen him, as he had done absolutely nothing to win her over. She had been the one who took the first step. She stayed up late talking that evening at his mother's house, after Tadeu had left. It was she who always found ways to touch his arm whenever possible. She had even initiated their first kiss. Beto would not have been foolish enough to refuse a kiss from Cintia. He would never miss the opportunity to kiss such a beautiful woman.

At times, he even thought she wanted the relationship to become more serious, but she hid that desire well, portraying herself as a modern woman, unlike others, one who was content with casual encounters. Beto always thought that all women were eager for a relationship, to get married, and have children right after the first kiss. He believed that women were dependent on men and would do anything to keep a good partner.

Beto considered himself an expert in understanding women.

That evening, the three of them met at a pizza place, one of the few in town. Tadeu felt awkward, looking at Cintia and remembering her wandering around his house.

He had seen her in pajamas, disheveled, just waking up. Granted, it wasn't necessarily *this* Cintia, but somehow he felt he knew her better than Beto did. He knew she liked to run to relieve stress, spent an inordinate amount of time brushing her teeth, and that when she had nightmares, she remained scared for the rest of the night. Tadeu had watched her sleep countless times. He also knew that during the week she avoided sweets and fried foods, but on weekends, she allowed herself to indulge in something delicious, her greatest weakness being dark chocolate.

On many occasions, he had heard her talking to the other Tadeu about her work routine: arriving at the clinic at nine, having lunch at a nearby restaurant—one where she knew the owner well enough to pay her bill monthly. After work, she went straight to the gym and, to save time, showered there before heading home late, spending time with her cats, watching a movie, sipping a glass of wine, and reading before bed (though she wasn't following any particular book at the moment). She called Beatriz almost daily, worried about her mother's fragile health.

They ordered a large pizza and three beers. The waiter took their order and promptly brought the drinks. They toasted to a new phase, to the renewal of the friendship between Beto and Tadeu, and to Beto's promises to visit his mother more often.

They toasted because they were young and had their entire lives ahead of them.

Nevertheless, Tadeu hadn't fully relaxed. He couldn't help but notice Cintia's affectionate gestures, trying to hold Beto's hand, though he always managed to free it after a few seconds. She kissed him on the cheek, and he responded with a forced smile, the kind people give when posing for an unwanted photograph. Beto only loosened up after a few beers, eventually showing her more affection. At one point, he brushed a strand of hair from her face and gave her a brief kiss on the neck. She blushed, enjoying being treated well. She deserved to be treated well.

At the end of the night, they split the bill evenly and paid the waiter. However, they lingered at the table for a while longer; there was still some beer left.

* * * * *

Tadeu had developed a new habit. Before entering the house, he pressed his ear against the door, listening for any sound that might indicate that someone was inside. After his recent encounter with the other Cintia, he had become more apprehensive; he didn't want to come face-to-face with his "new "guests". For this reason, he also started leaving Max outside. He had arranged a wooden doghouse to protect him from the weather. The house was on the porch, sheltered by a roof and surrounded by walls, ensuring that Max wouldn't get wet or cold.

Tadeu crossed the garden, stepped onto the porch, and pressed his ear to the door. Every time he heard noises inside the house, he preferred to sit outside and wait until the voices subsided. The only problem was that after several consecutive days of doing this, nosy Odete had begun to notice. The woman would stay inside her house with the curtain slightly open, observing. She was so peculiar that she didn't even bother to greet him, despite knowing that Tadeu was aware of her presence. She simply didn't care.

But today, there was only silence.

All clear. He could go inside.

That weekend, he didn't encounter anyone at home. *Did they go on a trip?* he thought, chuckling to himself. It was common for couples to take weekend trips, and there were many places to visit in the region. When the weather was warm, they could enjoy the nearby waterfalls. During the colder seasons, there were beautiful farm hotels in the area, ranging from simple to luxurious. He would be thrilled to take Cintia to one of those hotels for a weekend.

For now, though, Tadeu took advantage of finally being alone. It had been a few years since he'd indulged in anything illicit, but he still had a joint hidden somewhere in his closet. He lit it, took a deep drag, and closed his eyes. He exhaled a thick cloud of smoke. He was trying to relax; lately, his life had become chaotic. Sitting on the couch, he spent long minutes staring at the ceiling, contemplating its whiteness and attempting to clear his mind. Yet his thoughts always returned to Cintia. By this time, she was likely lying in bed, exchanging affectionate messages with Beto, wishing him goodnight. If he were her boyfriend, Tadeu would be doing exactly the same thing.

He lamented feeling so inferior. He had always led a life without grand plans, but now he felt the urge to change. Observing his other life, he realized how he could do things differently. If only he weren't so weak and intimidated by Beto and his successful career, he might have approached Cintia first. He had always been insecure, never having fallen in love like this before. The other Tadeu was far more confident, dressed in trendier clothes, and had a more modern haircut. The other Cintia wanted to be with that guy, not with him. He was tired of feeling sorry for himself. This was the push he needed to decide to change. He wasn't sure where to start, but he would begin. He would watch the other Tadeu and learn from him.

He fell asleep right there on the couch.

# Fourteen

Tadeu woke up to the sound of the door being opened. The other couple had finally returned home. They ignored his presence on the couch, chatting animatedly. The other Tadeu hugged the other Cintia around the waist, kissed her, and said weekends were always better with her by his side. Tadeu paid attention to the details, noticing the other Tadeu's neatly pressed shirt, perfectly-fitting jeans, and brand-new sneakers. He also saw a car key clipped to the other Tadeu's belt. In this version of reality, Tadeu didn't own a car, but apparently, the other Tadeu did.

Tadeu had noticed before that the other Tadeu's furniture was better—nothing extravagant, but of noticeably higher quality. His own belongings were mostly hand-me-downs from when his parents lived in the house. Meanwhile, this other version of himself seemed to be successful. He had enough money to afford nicer things, and surely that had given him the confidence to approach a woman like Cintia.

Tadeu wasn't sure yet how he would learn more about the other version of himself, but he knew he had to figure it out. He was tired of being himself. He even considered interacting with the other Tadeu, just as he had managed to interact with Cintia. But he wasn't sure if that was a good idea. It might scare the other Tadeu and cause confusion.

As Tadeu pondered these thoughts, a darker idea crossed his mind: returning to selling drugs. It had been a quick and easy way to make money before, and he had been good at it. Maybe it was the only thing he was good at.

Determined to study the other version of himself more closely, Tadeu began paying attention to the details—like the car key clipped to the belt. He decided to turn this strange situation into a learning experience, especially since he had little else to do.

As time passed, he absorbed more and more information. He noticed that the other Tadeu used his phone far more often than he did, always typing or talking. Was it work-related? Whatever the job was, it must be important. Only important people received work calls and messages after hours. One day, a specific phone conversation piqued Tadeu's curiosity. He overheard the other Tadeu discussing delivery deadlines and mentioning "a car arriving in a few hours", though what it all meant was still unclear.

Since the incident where the other Cintia interacted with him, Tadeu had become more cautious. He only stayed close to the other couple when he was sure he wouldn't be seen. He soon noticed a pattern: during the week, the other Tadeu was often alone, with Cintia only appearing on weekends. It was clear that they were in a long-distance relationship, but they seemed to manage it without much difficulty. However, Tadeu never overheard them discussing long-term plans. Perhaps it was still too early in their relationship for that.

* * * * *

One morning, while sweeping the living room, Tadeu felt dizzy. He hadn't been eating properly for weeks, but he brushed it off. After throwing away the dust, he returned to the backyard, where he suddenly heard voices in the living room. Two male voices. Moving quietly, he approached the door to listen. The other Tadeu and the other Beto were in the middle of a conversation. That was new—he hadn't seen the other Beto in his hallucinations before. Now he knew they encountered each other in that scenario as well.

"What do you mean? Are you thinking of moving to the capital?" the other Beto asked.

"I am. Things with Cintia are getting serious, you know? It's tough only seeing her on weekends," replied the other Tadeu.

"And what does she think about that?" The other Beto's rational tone seemed to be trying to bring his friend back to reality.

"I haven't talked to her about it yet. I thought I'd surprise her. What do you think?"

"I don't think anything," Beto laughed. "I'd rather not give my opinion. You know me. Giving up everything for someone else is risky. You've only been together for a few months."

"Yeah, you're right," the other Tadeu admitted. "But I've spent my whole life here. I've saved a lot because I barely have any expenses. Starting over in the capital might be a good idea."

"And when are you thinking of moving?"

"I'm not sure yet. I need to decide what to do with the house. Who would want to rent or buy a property in the middle of nowhere? I could keep it, but I don't want the hassle. Houses can be a lot of trouble."

"Well, it sounds like a good plan. I think Cintia will be happy. Are you two doing well?"

"We are, yeah. And if we get married, your mom will be the maid of honor! " The other Tadeu laughed, referencing how Ivone had introduced him to Cintia the previous Christmas.

The conversation revealed more than Tadeu had expected. The other Beto seemed identical to the Beto he knew, successful in every life. Why did some people get all the luck? It was becoming clear that if Tadeu wanted to succeed in life and win over a woman like Cintia, it wouldn't happen by continuing on his current path.

The other Beto got up to leave, mentioning that he needed to pick up groceries for his mother. Just as he was getting ready to go, his phone rang.

"Hi, yeah, I can talk," he said. "I'm at a friend's house... I should be back by Monday. I can't afford to miss work this week... Alright, it's a date."

"Who was that?" the other Tadeu asked.

"Aline, a girl I've been seeing. She wants to go out again."

"Oh, really? You didn't mention her before. Is she pretty? Nice? Maybe this time someone will really catch your attention," he teased.

"She's normal," the other Beto said. "I like her. We're not dating, but we've been hanging out a lot. She's nice, works at the same company, different department."
After this, the other Beto left.

* * * * *

Now Tadeu understood why the other Cintia hadn't ended up with the other Beto. He was already seeing someone—Aline. Ivone might have introduced Cintia to him with the best intentions, but the other Beto was already involved with someone, and it seemed to be serious. Though he wouldn't admit it, the other Beto seemed to like Aline.
Perplexed by all this new information, Tadeu decided to go for a walk. "Enough for today," he thought. He walked through the kitchen, opened the door to the laundry room, and let it close behind him.
Hearing the noise, the other Tadeu called out, "Who's there?" He walked to the laundry room but found nothing except a closed door.

# Fifteen

Tadeu decided to walk to the city square, the same one where the New Year's party had taken place, and then he sat on a bench, observing the city's life unfold. Every day, he discovered new things about his supposed other life, and needed to learn how to deal with them.

Night began to cover the sky, now a dark grayish-blue. The damp weather moistened the foliage, and children played on the lawn. Tadeu approached an old man selling cotton candy and asked for some. Out of nowhere, he felt a craving for it. How long had it been since he had eaten something sweet? He savored each pink piece for a long time. He wondered if Cintia liked cotton candy.

He arrived home late, and there was no one there—at least, he didn't see anyone. He turned on the TV and picked any movie on the schedule. It would be great to watch a movie on a modern plasma TV like the other Tadeu. He fell asleep right there.

He woke up to Max barking outside. It had been a while since he let the dog sleep inside, and Max, indignant, always made a scene to wake him up. He went out onto the balcony, realizing that he had slept in yesterday's clothes. It was very early, and he hadn't even reached his usual waking time for work. He hadn't bought food in days; the fridge was empty, and he had been eating out, poorly and sporadically. He went back inside, washed his face, brushed his teeth, grabbed a coat, and walked to the bakery.

Since it was very early, the bakery was still empty. The delightful smell of bread filled the entire space. The owner was finishing organizing things at the cash register, and a few employees were already bustling about. Tadeu decided to treat himself to a hearty breakfast that day: he ordered coffee with milk, toast with scrambled eggs, and ham. He sat at one of the empty tables and picked up a random newspaper from the stack of publications.

While reading the local news—nothing particularly surprising—he heard Odete entering the place. The old woman, as grumpy as ever, didn't even respond to the employees' greetings. Tadeu focused on a headline reporting that the police had arrested another drug dealer in the area, lamenting the complexities of the war on drugs. The server brought Tadeu's order and smiled graciously.

"Here you go," she said.

He savored the scrambled eggs with gusto. The latte was excellent, too. He missed the breakfasts he used to have with his stepmother at this same bakery. When he was a child, Márcia always let him choose a sweet treat while she bought bread.

He pushed the empty plate to the edge of the table and finished reading the local society news. He found amusement in the photos of his old troublemaking friends, now posing with their perfect families—men who, just a few years ago, cheated on their then-girlfriends and current wives with women from neighboring towns. Men who used cocaine while gambling money in poker games and later returned home, shamelessly boasting. They accompanied their mothers to church and, of course, agreed on the importance of following the Christian path.

Tadeu felt a bit disgusted, realizing that the same guys who used to come to his house looking for drugs now passed him on the street as if they didn't even know him. But he couldn't condemn them; they didn't have a choice. In general, they were kids of wealthy but crude farmers who considered it perfectly normal to take their sons to brothels to "lose their virginity like real men".

It was time to go home. He still needed to buy some groceries, and had work to do.

Tadeu was next in line at the cash and had glanced at the clock numerous times. Odete, who was currently being served, kept picking on the cashier, accusing her of doing everything wrong. She left so disgruntled with the poor girl that she grabbed her bags from the counter angrily, stomping loudly to make her displeasure known. Tadeu watched the old lady with a somewhat mischievous desire to laugh when Odete tripped on the stairs and fell, scattering all her purchases around.

There was an enormous urge to leave her there, fallen and cursing, but the peer pressure of the other customers' stares forced Tadeu to offer help. While he picked up the groceries, Odete brushed her hands against her dress, trying to clean off the dust and muttering curses unfit for a good Christian. When he noticed that the old lady had scraped her knee badly, Tadeu felt a bit sorry for her. She tried to get up, but her knee hurt too much. Feeling awkward, Tadeu offered assistance. Odete hesitated for a moment, but with no other choice, reluctantly accepted his help.

Tadeu walked down the slope, carrying the groceries and supporting the elderly woman, who moved at a slower pace than usual. When they reached her house, Tadeu hesitated, wondering whether to offer to come inside. He had never been inside Odete's house before. They had been neighbors for years, but the closest he had come was to retrieve soccer balls that had landed in her yard. Out of politeness, he thought it best to ask.

"Do you want help with putting away the groceries?"

"Yes," the old lady replied grumpily. Not even when she needed help could she manage to be friendly.

Tadeu entered the living room and immediately felt a stifling heat and a strong smell of mustiness mixed with dust. Everything was closed: doors, windows, the entire room immersed in darkness. On the shelves were hundreds of images of saints and Jesus Christ, with extinguished candles and rosaries wrapped around them. A piano in the corner added to the eerie atmosphere.

He settled the old lady on the couch, then went to the kitchen. After rummaging through the mess, he managed to find some ice, a bowl of water, napkins, and a dish towel. Back in the living room, he carefully cleaned her scraped knee, wrapped the ice in the towel, and applied pressure to the wound. "Now hold this here, okay? You banged your knee pretty hard, but the pain will pass soon."

Odete looked Tadeu squarely in the eyes, seeming surprised by his kindness.

"Thank you, young man, but I think I can take care of myself. You can go now."

"No problem. If you need anything, feel free to call me," he said, purely out of politeness. She didn't even have his phone number. He looked around for the groceries. They were on the floor near the front door. He picked up the bags, but before he could take a step, Odete stopped him.

"Wait a moment... I need one last favor."

"Of course you do," he muttered, rolling his eyes.

"I need to take some medicine, but I can't manage to climb the stairs right now. Could you please fetch it for me? It's upstairs in the bathroom."

Her house was the largest on the street, the only one with two floors.

"Sure, what's the name of the medicine?" he asked.

"It's in a box, like a pill organizer, you know? The box is orange."

Tadeu left the groceries on the coffee table and climbed the staircase, sighing. Upstairs, he was faced with three doors: two slightly ajar and the third closed. From what he could see, one room was the master bedroom and the other seemed to be some sort of office. The third door, the closed one, was likely the bathroom.

He turned the handle and found a multitude of medications, containers, and creams scattered over the sink. The mirror was worn at the edges, resembling something out of a horror movie, and Tadeu was half-expecting to see a ghostly figure at any moment. The tiles were tacky, in an outdated shade of brown, and even the bidet boasted a hideous color. He opened the drawers. It was challenging to locate anything in that chaos—a plethora of hair products, clips, brushes, and shower caps.

Finally, he found the medicine on a shelf below the mirror. It seemed to be for high blood pressure, one of those ailments that affected most elderly people. Unable to resist his curiosity, he began peeking into the other rooms. This house had been the stage for many stories invented by the neighborhood children, and Tadeu could hardly believe he was there.

Odete's bedroom displayed a horrific combination of colors; the suede fabric curtains were moss green, and the duvet had a floral pattern that he imagined dated back to at least the seventies.

The carpet made the atmosphere feel heavy. It seemed as though Tadeu had traveled back in time and entered a house from decades ago.

"Is everything alright up there?" Odete shouted suspiciously from downstairs.

"Yes, it took some time for me to find your medication, but I'm coming down now," he replied.

Before stepping onto the stairs, he glanced one last time into the third room. The place was filled with dark wooden shelves, many old and yellowed books, stacks of newspapers, magazine clippings, and recipe books. On top of a large, heavy chest, something caught his eye: a typewriter, whose sole purpose seemed to be gathering dust. It was better to come down soon, or it would be too obvious that he was snooping around the house.

He fetched a glass of water from the kitchen and offered it to Odete with her pill. She took a tiny sip and left the rest on the table. With a deep sigh, she said, "Maybe I haven't formed a fair image of you."

"How so?" Tadeu asked.

"You and your friends from the neighborhood, when you were kids, made my life miserable with your shouting, balls flying everywhere. Then you grew up and turned into a bunch of rebellious teenagers, drinking beer and leaving bottles on the street. I never liked that behavior, but I always imagined it was because of the poor upbringing your father gave you."

That old bat had no filter whatsoever, Tadeu thought.

"Maybe I never showed my best side to you either, but what could I do? I was just a kid, and you never made much effort to be nice either," he teased with a hint of irony, ending with a friendly chuckle to soften the tone.

"I never did, indeed. There's no one in this town worth the effort. The only person I care for is Ivone. Your stepmother... Márcia, I liked that girl, too, but your father wouldn't leave her alone. It was hard for us to even meet for a simple tea."

"What do you mean, meet for a simple tea? Were you two friends?"

"We weren't close friends, but were neighbors and would chat from time to time. You don't know this, but when you were very little, your stepmother often had to go to the supermarket and left me to take care of you."

"Really? How come I never knew about this?"

"Because she didn't tell your father. Everything Márcia did away from him was kept secret. He could never predict his reactions. On many occasions, he beat her for no apparent reason, so she preferred never to go into details about what she did."

"It's very sad that you know these bad stories about my family. Actually, it's quite shameful to me that the whole neighborhood witnessed that horrible marriage."

"My dear, this town is full of failed marriages, of sad, frustrated people, of petty human beings. Just look at how disgusting those social columns are, filled with people rich in money yet so poor in spirit."

For the first time in a long while, Tadeu heard someone speak something coherent, and he never expected that person to be Odete, of all people. She let out a long sigh, closed and opened her eyes, and continued:

"I live here because I inherited my father's house. I grew up in a family where women couldn't work or achieve independence. They arranged a marriage for me when I was very young, around nineteen years old, but my husband left me as soon as I found out I couldn't have children. After all, I wasn't fulfilling my role in society. It was pointless to have a wife who couldn't give him multiple heirs. I was left alone, all my married friends with dozens of children, all raised perfectly, just as society expects a woman to do. Soon, they all turned their backs on me. Who would want to be friends with a spinster who can't find a husband?"

53

## Sixteen

Odete's vulnerability hung in the air, and Tadeu was still processing the gravity of it all. He had never imagined the bitter woman who terrified him and his friends as children had carried so much pain. In her story, he saw echoes of his own life, where bitterness masked unspoken sorrow.

Behind someone bitter, there's always a sad story. It was true for him, and apparently true for her, too.

When he was younger, Odete had simply been the "witch of the street", the cranky neighbor who yelled at them for playing too loud. Now, seeing her like this, he understood why. The absence of a child in her marriage had ruined her life. Why would she like children when their noise reminded her of her own loss? Besides, nobody was obligated to tolerate noisy, mischievous kids.

"Wow, Odete," Tadeu finally spoke. "I had no idea about all of this. What a sad story. I'm really sorry."

"Don't be sorry," she said, waving off his sympathy. "I could have left here, started over from scratch, lived my life. I love playing the piano, and I play very well. If I had the courage, I could have gone out there, performed in bars, music venues, maybe even become famous."

"I've never heard you play the piano."

"It's been many years since I've played at all. The thought of those keys only brings me the sadness of remembering the life I could have had but didn't." Her gaze softened as it drifted to the corner where the piano sat, covered in dust. She sighed. "But it's too late now. I'm old, sick, and with each passing day, I get closer to death."

"Don't say that," Tadeu tried to lift her spirits. "I thought you enjoyed helping at the church. From what I hear, the bingo events you organize are famous for being the best."

"The church is a pastime, a way to keep myself from going crazy. I've always had a lot of faith, you know? But lately, I've been doubting many things, and even my faith is in question."

Tadeu glanced at his phone. He had already missed the time to go to work. He quickly sent a message, explaining that he'd only come in the afternoon because he was helping an injured person.

"Tadeu," Odete said, her tone suddenly serious. "Don't let others decide your life for you. Don't become an embittered old person like me."

"Why are you saying this?" Tadeu asked, caught off-guard.

"I see you, day after day, locked up at home, without friends, without hobbies, without a woman to share life with. I have nothing left to do in this life. The window of my living room is my television. I know everyone's schedules, the whole street's routine. You live almost directly across from my house, and apart from that unbearable mutt of yours, no one else ever comes in."

Tadeu couldn't argue. "That's true. Unfortunately, I haven't been as lucky as Beto, who went to the capital, studied, and now works at a big company."

"It's never too late to start over," she said, her voice unexpectedly soft. "You're still very young. There's still time to leave, to get something better than living here, on this cobblestone street, in this town full of people who don't care about you. Don't become neighbors with sad old ladies like me."

Tadeu swallowed hard. Her words struck a chord deep inside him. He didn't know what to say. Odete pressed the ice pack against her swollen knee, her eyes half-closed as she settled into the sofa.

"After my father died," Tadeu began, not sure why he was opening up, "and after I took care of my stepmother until she passed away too, I lost all motivation. It's like all my energy to do something better with my life drained away."

Odete looked at him for a moment before speaking, her voice gentler than ever. "I understand that. But don't let that be the end of your story, Tadeu. There's still time for you to write a new chapter." Tadeu listened intently, feeling the weight of Odete's words settle heavily around him. He had never expected this glimpse into his father's life, into the unraveling of a man he barely understood.

"There was no joy in achieving things without anyone to share them with," he said quietly. "I ended up just drifting around, staying in my father's house, and, well, you know my problems." He referred to the time he had been caught by the police. Odete had probably watched everything unfold from her little window.

"What saddened me the most was seeing Márcia lose her spark," Odete said, her gaze distant, as if she were digging up memories from the past.

"How so?" Tadeu prompted.

"She was such a beautiful woman, so full of life and joy. Over time, Walmir sucked out everything good in her; his madness destroyed both him and her."

"The alcohol, you mean?"

"Alcohol was a consequence, not the reason your father ended up like he did. Your father was a strong man, someone who stood out." Odete paused, gathering her thoughts, and then continued, her voice steady yet tinged with sadness. "Tadeu, I've never told anyone this, but I believe you're old enough to hear it without any problems. Many times, from my little window here, I saw your father talking to himself. I watched him pacing around the house, gesturing as if he were arguing with someone. Often, he would clutch his temples, tightly shut his eyes, grit his teeth, or cover his ears with his hands and run out of the house. Sometimes he would sit on the porch for hours."

Tadeu felt a chill run down his spine. The image of his father lost in his own mind was haunting. "It didn't take long before he started drinking," Odete continued. "Before I knew it, he was coming home drunk every day. He argued with Márcia, saying nonsensical things, accusing her of being with other men, talking to other people, bringing lovers into the house. It was madness; the woman was a saint."

Tadeu settled into the armchair, elbows resting on his knees, deeply absorbed in this unheard perspective. If he hadn't helped the old lady with her scraped knee, she would never have opened up like this, and he would have lived without knowing the truth.

It was stuffy inside the house, and the stories about his father made him sweat even more. He felt beads of perspiration forming on his forehead and discreetly wiped them away with the back of his hand. He looked around, noting the lack of even a fan. How could Odete endure such a place?

"One day, I heard Márcia crying in the garden," she continued. "I went to ask what was happening, if everything was okay. Sobbing, she confided in me that her marriage was falling apart, that she didn't know what to do anymore, that Walmir was also hearing and seeing things. She didn't bring men into the house—she was terrified of his reaction—but he swore up and down that he always saw her with someone. She told me she didn't understand if it was a trick on his part to provoke her into asking for a divorce. She always knew that he had only truly loved your mother."

Tadeu was stunned. As if the chaos his life had become in recent months wasn't enough, now this bombshell weighed heavily on him. He didn't know where to begin organizing his thoughts.

The heat in the house became unbearable; he needed to get out. Sweat trickled down his back, suffocating him. He glanced at the clock and turned to Odete. "May I leave now?"

"Of course," she replied, gratitude etched on her face. "Thank you again for your help. I'm sorry for my outburst."

"I don't know what made me talk so much!" Odete added with a hint of embarrassment.

Tadeu managed a small smile, but inside he felt a storm brewing, a mixture of anger, sadness, and a desperate need to understand the fractured history of his family. As he stepped outside, the fresh air hit him like a wave, and he realized that he had a lot to process.

# Seventeen

Tadeu paced back and forth in his living room, his mind racing as he pieced together the tragic puzzle of his father's life. The possibility that had begun to flicker in his thoughts now seemed like the only explanation. His father, Walmir, had been suffering from hallucinations—seeing people who weren't there, voices that didn't exist. It all made sense now. The accusations of infidelity, the late-night drinking, the unpredictable rage—it wasn't just alcoholism or jealousy; his father was battling something far deeper, something he likely couldn't understand himself.

Tadeu could hardly breathe, the weight of this revelation pressing down on him. His father had been raised in a simple, uneducated environment, where talking about mental health was unheard of. There was no one Walmir could have confided in, no one who would have believed him. And in his confusion, he had turned to violence and alcohol, trying to escape from the torment in his mind. But there was no escape—only the destruction of his own life, along with Márcia's, and the young family he had tried to build.

Tadeu stopped pacing and stood still, staring out the window but seeing nothing. For the first time, he felt an overwhelming wave of pity for his father. Walmir wasn't just the violent drunk he had always resented. He was a man who had lost control of his reality, suffering in silence for years, unable to seek help. Tadeu's heart clenched as he imagined the terror his father must have felt, seeing visions that no one else could, not knowing if he was losing his mind or if he was being deceived by his own senses.

But as much as he pitied his father, Tadeu's thoughts quickly shifted to Márcia. She had come into this mess with nothing but good intentions, offering support to Walmir and raising a child who wasn't her own. She had done nothing to deserve the cruelty that life had thrown at her, the beatings, the accusations, the unbearable burden of living with a man slowly unraveling. And yet, despite it all, she had stayed. Tadeu's chest tightened with grief. He had always loved her, but now that love was mixed with guilt and sorrow. How had she endured all of this without ever complaining? Without ever asking for more than the few moments of peace she could find?

He slumped onto the sofa, head in his hands. The image of Márcia crying in the garden, confiding in Odete that she didn't know what to do, flashed through his mind. She had been so trapped, unable to leave, unable to save herself or her marriage. All she had was the knowledge that she was raising a child—and even that had become a burden in the chaos Walmir had brought into their home.

Tadeu took a deep breath. He couldn't change the past, couldn't undo the years of suffering that had plagued his family. But the truth, painful as it was, gave him a new perspective. His father had been a victim of his own mind, not the heartless villain he had always thought. And Márcia—she was the unsung hero, the one who had endured it all with a strength Tadeu could barely comprehend. As much as he wanted to resent his father, Tadeu realized that anger wouldn't serve him anymore. What he felt now was a deep sadness, an ache that reached into the core of his being. He couldn't help but wonder how different his life—and theirs—could have been if someone had understood Walmir's condition earlier. If someone had intervened, could they have had a chance at happiness? Could they have lived without the constant shadow of mistrust, fear, and madness?

Tadeu wiped the sweat from his brow and stood up. He couldn't stay in this room, in this house, surrounded by the ghosts of the past. He needed to clear his head, to figure out what to do next. For too long, he had drifted through life, paralyzed by the weight of his family's history. But now, for the first time, he felt the stirrings of something different—a need to move forward, to escape the trap that had caught his father, Márcia, and even himself.

He knew what Odete had said was true: it wasn't too late to start over. But first, he needed to confront the truth, to come to terms with the pain and the suffering that had shaped his life. It was the only way that he could begin to heal.

# Eighteen

Cintia was glowing with happiness. Her job in the bustling capital was flourishing, and she was gaining recognition for her hard work and dedication. She had found a rhythm in the fast-paced city life, and every day felt like a new adventure. But beyond her professional success, there was something even more exhilarating in her life—Beto.

Beto was everything Cintia admired in a man. He was driven, intelligent, and kind, with a wit that never failed to make her smile. Overtime, their connection deepened. Though they hadn't yet defined their relationship, Cintia felt confident that it was only a matter of time before Beto fully opened up to her. His occasional affectionate gestures and the way he looked at her with admiration told her all she needed to know.

She was patient. Cintia wasn't one to rush things—especially something as important as love. She knew Beto was cautious, hesitant. She had the feeling it had something to do with his past—a past she knew very little about. She kept asking him questions, trying to learn more about who he was. What had his life been like when he left home and started college? Had he been a good student? The kind of guy who went out a lot? Drank? A womanizer? What had his relationships with friends been like? It was a challenge for her, but she believed that one day, she'd get to know him on a deeper level. And she also believed in the undeniable chemistry they shared. Every time they spent the evening talking about their dreams, sharing stories over dinner, or enjoying a walk through the vibrant city streets, Cintia could feel him drawing closer.

She admired his ambition. Beto was successful in his own right, having worked his way up in a competitive field. He had recently secured a high profile position at a well-known company, and Cintia couldn't help but feel proud of him. They both understood the pressures of their careers, which only brought them closer, united by their shared experiences.

Her friends noticed her happiness. They often teased her, saying she was glowing like someone deeply in love, and though she laughed it off, they weren't entirely wrong. Cintia was falling for Beto, and she believed he was falling for her, too. She was confident that once he fully opened his heart, they would be inseparable.

Cintia smiled to herself as she thought about him. She was already imagining the future they could build together, traveling, supporting each other's dreams, and maybe even starting a family someday. She didn't want to rush Beto, but she was sure of one thing: when the time was right, he would realize that she was the woman he had been waiting for all along.

For now, she was content to enjoy the present, savoring each moment they spent together, knowing that their bond was growing stronger with every shared experience.

Cintia felt her heart flutter as she opened the door, and there was Beto, looking a little tired from his long day but still managing to give her that shy smile that always melted her. His eyes lit up when he saw her, and the kiss he planted on her lips, though soft, was enough to make her feel the warmth of his presence.

"Sorry I'm late," Beto said as he stepped inside, loosening his tie. "That meeting took forever."

She smiled, closing the door behind him. "No problem at all. I figured you'd be tired, so I made something simple, spaghetti *aglio e olio*. Hope you're hungry."

His eyes widened with appreciation as the aroma of garlic, olive oil, and chili filled the air. "It smells amazing. You're spoiling me."

She laughed, handing him a glass of wine. "Maybe a little. But you deserve it after a day like that."

They made their way to the small dining table she had set up, candles flickering softly in the dim light, giving the room an intimate glow. Cintia couldn't help but steal glances at Beto as he sat down, looking at ease, yet there was always something restrained about him. It was one of the things she found intriguing about him—he wasn't like the others. He didn't rush things, didn't try to overwhelm her with charm or slick lines. He seemed real, and it gave her hope that this might actually be something worth holding onto.

As they began to eat, Cintia felt a familiar nervousness creep in. It was hard for her not to compare her past with her present, and she couldn't help but think of her ex-boyfriend—the one who had left her broken and wary of trusting again. But with Beto, things were different. He was kind, respectful, and never pushed her boundaries. It was a breath of fresh air, and yet, that same patience and restraint made her wonder if he felt as strongly about her as she did about him.

"So," she began, swirling her wine in her glass, "how's work going? You seem busier than usual lately."

Beto leaned back, relaxing into his chair. "Yeah, things have been crazy. We're in the middle of a big project, and the deadlines are tight. But," he paused, looking at her with a grateful smile, "coming here makes it all worth it."

Cintia felt her heart skip a beat. His words, simple as they were, made her feel seen, appreciated. Maybe it was the wine loosening her up, or maybe it was the fact that she was tired of waiting for him to make the first move, but she decided to be bolder than usual.

"I'm glad you feel that way," she said, her voice soft but sure. "Because I like having you here. More than I've let on."

Beto's eyes met hers, and for a moment, the air between them felt charged. She saw something shift in his expression, something warmer and more open than she had seen before.

"I like being here, too," he admitted, his voice low and sincere. "A lot more than I thought I would."

Cintia smiled, feeling a rush of relief. For so long, she'd been holding back, afraid that pushing too hard would scare him away, but now, sitting across from him, the distance between them felt smaller than ever.

They continued to eat, the conversation flowing easily as always, but there was an unspoken understanding now—something more was there, something worth exploring. And for the first time in a long time, Cintia felt safe enough to let herself believe that maybe, just maybe, this could be something real.

* * * * *

While Cintia served the dishes, Beto was busy on his phone, responding to work emails he didn't want to leave until the next day. "Beto, come on... put down your phone for a bit. Let's talk, let's eat," she urged.

"Just a sec, I just need to send this... There, sent. Now I'm all yours!" he said with a grin.

It was difficult to get his attention sometimes. Still, Cintia thought it was better than being with someone idle who didn't enjoy working. After all, she worked hard herself, and appreciated men who valued that. She twirled a forkful of pasta, savoring the aroma.

"And how about you? How was your day?" she asked.

"Nothing special—meetings, clients, charts, coffee... lots of coffee. I've been working on that project I just told you about, under the usual pressure my bosses always put on me. Office routine, nothing exciting," Beto replied with a shrug. "You know, Beto, I've been thinking... What if we organize a dinner with some of my friends and their husbands? We could have a couples' night with plenty of food and board games... I love board games!" she suggested, her eyes lighting up.

"Really? I'm not sure... I feel a bit awkward trying to fit in with those guys I don't know. They'll probably start talking about football, and I'll have to pretend to be interested just so I don't leave them hanging. Then the conversation won't last long, and we'll end up in that awkward silence. Afterward, they'll probably leave here talking badly about me to their girlfriends."

"Oh, come on, Beto! I just thought we could have some fun in a different way. You're so intelligent; I don't know why my friends' husbands wouldn't like you."

"Because no one does, trust me... You're just plain crazy for liking me," he retorted, laughing and teasing.

"I'm a bit crazy, yes, and now you'll just have to put up with me." She smiled back.

They finished dinner, washed and put away the dishes, then poured more wine before settling on the couch to watch a movie. Cintia, feeling a bit chilly, wrapped herself in a quilt. Normally, at this hour, Beto would be out with his friends at some chic bar in the city. He enjoyed going out with his coworkers, all dressed in suits and ties, drawing the attention of the women around. With a glass of whiskey in hand, it never took long before he caught the eye of some intriguing woman, exchanging subtle, inviting glances. The night didn't always end with him taking someone home, but the thrill of the chase was already a victory in itself. He loved the seduction phase; once he got what he wanted, the appeal quickly faded. Women who were too easy weren't his type. He believed that if they were too available to him, they'd be just as available to anyone else. A woman like that? He would never even consider marrying her.

He enjoyed Cintia's company; she was pleasant, and their relationship had been going well for a few months. However, he still didn't feel comfortable enough to meet her friends, let alone engage in conversations about football. To him, football was a tremendous waste of time. He preferred to spend his free time studying, reading, and taking online courses. He didn't like it at all when Cintia pushed things between them; he preferred to let their relationship develop naturally. Suddenly, his phone emitted a short tone, and Beto quickly pulled it from his pocket, his demeanor tense.

"Again, Beto?"

"Sorry, baby girl, but I really need to see what this is," he replied. Cintia melted every time he called her "baby girl", and he knew it well.

"Give me that phone; I'll tell your boss to leave you alone," she said, furrowing her brow in a playful tone. She reached for the phone, not expecting him to grip it tightly. When she exerted more force, the phone slipped from her hand and landed on the living room carpet.

On the screen, she caught a glimpse of the message he was typing: "I'm still here with her, not sure until what time..."

That seemed strange; it didn't sound like a message to a boss at all. Beto held her hands to stop her from grabbing the phone and quickly retrieved it.

"Beto... what's this message about? Who are you talking to?"

"No one, it's work stuff, I told you."

"Work stuff? Your boss wants to know until what time you'll be here with me? What kind of boss is that?"

"I needed to submit a report early tomorrow morning and promised to finish it tonight... So I said I wouldn't have time because I was with my girlfriend," he tried to convince her.

The word "girlfriend" sounded like music to Cintia's ears, making her forget all her suspicions. How could a woman in love be so vulnerable? It seemed impossible that Beto had such control over her.

"Girlfriend? I'm your girlfriend?" Her eyes sparkled.

"Seems like it."

He set the phone down and kissed her, wrapping his arms around her waist. Her heart raced. But just before the glow from the phone screen faded, she caught a glimpse of a name in the notification: Aline.

# Nineteen

This weekend, Cintia arrived in the countryside alone after Beatriz called to let her know she wasn't feeling well. They had agreed that Cintia would take her to an emergency room in a nearby, larger city that had better facilities. Beatriz had been battling a fever and feeling unusually tired all week. Cintia felt a twinge of worry as she drove, hoping her mother would be okay. The tranquil countryside was a stark contrast to her anxious thoughts, and she couldn't help but wish she were there with Beto, sharing the peacefulness of the setting instead of rushing to a hospital.

Upon arriving in the neighboring city, Cintia typed "hospital" into the GPS to check their options. She selected one she had heard of before and followed the app's directions. Once they arrived, Beatriz was given priority treatment due to her age. The consultation was swift; the doctor diagnosed her with a simple virus. After administering IV fluids to help rehydrate her, he discharged Beatriz with a prescription and some advice for rest and recovery. Cintia felt relieved, grateful that it wasn't anything more serious. As they left the hospital, she promised Beatriz that she would take care of her and ensure that she had everything she needed.

For a while, Cintia stayed home taking care of her mother, making soup, and doing a bit of house maintenance. A few hours later, Beatriz fell asleep peacefully, the effects of the medication and exhaustion taking hold. Cintia left a note on the bedside table, telling her mother she would be back soon and to call her cell if anything was needed.

She then decided to go for a walk and, heading down the hill, arrived at the local bakery—the one everyone in the area goes to. She took a seat and ordered a Coke and a snack; it had been hours since she'd last eaten. While waiting for her food, she sent a message to Beto, updating him on her mother's condition and the doctor's appointment. Cintia felt a mix of relief and worry, hoping Beatriz would recover quickly. Cintia was still somewhat suspicious about the message she had read on Beto's phone days earlier, but with each passing hour, She tried to think about it less. After all, she was happy. Looking toward the door, she saw Tadeu entering, smiled at him, and gestured for him to come closer. "Where's Beto?" he asked as soon as he approached the table.

"This weekend he didn't want to come, so I came to take care of my sick mother instead. It was easier this way."

"Oh, is she feeling better?"

"Yes, she is. It wasn't anything serious, just a simple flu."

Tadeu decided to sit down with Cintia and ordered a coffee. As he glanced toward the door, he remembered the fall Odete had taken the other day. Now that she had recovered, they could laugh about it.

They chatted about various topics, but inevitably, the conversation shifted toward relationships. Tadeu was eager to know how things were going with Beto.

"We're officially dating now. It's serious," Cintia said, blushing.

"Well, that's a story to tell the grandchildren. Ivone will be happy. It was all she wanted lately, and she's managed to achieve her goal perfectly," he joked.

Cintia finished her snack and ordered a cappuccino. The conversation was so pleasant, she could have stayed there for hours.

"I never would have imagined that one day I'd be sitting here, chatting and having coffee with you. The day we met, I didn't really like you," she admitted.

"Oh, really? What did I do wrong?"

"You didn't do anything wrong, per se, but you arrived just when I was alone with Beto. It kind of ruined the mood." She looked down shyly. "I thought, 'Oh, why did this guy have to show up right now?'"

"Well, accept my apologies. They're late, but still sincere."

"Of course," she laughed softly. "In the end, everything turned out fine. It would've been complicated if we didn't like each other. Beto really appreciates you, especially for everything you do for his mother."

"I guess there wouldn't be any reason for us not to like each other."

"Yeah, maybe. It was my prejudice, I think."

"Prejudice? What do you mean? I don't understand."

"It's nothing." She hesitated for a moment, clearly regretful for letting the remark slip. "It's just that... I had heard some things about you and, well, I kind of didn't warm up to you at first." She finished the sentence with a friendly grimace. Even making funny faces, she looked beautiful.

"Things about me? I can imagine what it might be, but you should tell me so I can try to defend myself."

Cintia twirled the cup between her fingers, unsure of whether she should bring up the subject. It was in the past, and she didn't want to hurt anyone. Besides, she liked Tadeu; they had become good friends. Biting her lip, she continued.

"It's just that... I heard you had some trouble... with the police... with bad company... or something like that."

"Something like drugs? It's okay, you can talk about it. I don't mind discussing it with you," he replied calmly, as if tired of explaining the matter.

"Oh, it's just that... this was a big problem in my family. A very big problem."

"Why? Are they very conservative?"

"Not exactly. Do you remember that my uncle was the mayor here a long time ago?"

"Of course."

"So," she continued, "he was my mom's brother. His son, my cousin Pedro, started using drugs. At first, we thought it was just a phase—going to parties, smoking weed, getting drunk. But later, we found out he was using other things, you know?" She showed some embarrassment as she spoke. "My aunts and uncles didn't know what to do; they wanted to admit him to a psychiatric clinic."

"I understand... and how is he doing now?"

"Nowadays, he's doing better. We used to be close, but he became a different person. He was diagnosed with bipolar disorder, and the doctors said the drug use made it worse. He became depressed, withdrew from everyone. My uncle was so ashamed—how could the mayor deal with his son's issues publicly? No one wants to see their family's problems in the papers," she added with irony.

"I see."

"At the time, Pedro was sent to another city under the pretext of studying. They managed to hide it well. He lost so much weight, looked awful. I visited him once, but he was so drugged up he hardly recognized me. I felt really bad. I was young, and it was my first time seeing something like that up close, you know?"

"Unfortunately, it's more common than we realize."

"I know. And to make matters worse, my aunt and uncle couldn't agree on how to handle it. They blamed each other. My uncle said my aunt spoiled Pedro too much, and my aunt said my uncle was too strict, that Pedro just needed more attention and love. In the end, they separated. It was a nasty divorce—they probably still hate each other today."

"That's tough, I get it."

"Yeah... Well... And you? Why did you start using that stuff?" she asked, leaning forward and resting her elbows on the table.

"Rebellious teenager. Family problems. But nowadays, everything's fine. I never used anything too heavy—nothing that would destroy my life or make me sell things to fund the habit," he said with a small smile.

"I see... So those stories about you selling to others—are they just rumors?" Cintia asked, furrowing her brow, clearly interested.

"Who told you that?" Tadeu raised his eyebrows, a little surprised. He knew rumors had spread, but Cintia and her mother had only moved to the town recently, and the story was quite old.

"Beto mentioned it. Since we're dating, I kind of made him tell me everything."

Tadeu wasn't thrilled that Beto had shared this, but as he thought it over, he figured he might have done the same if he were in Beto's shoes.

# Twenty

Beto often thought Cintia visited her mother far too frequently. "Can't you go one Saturday without seeing the old lady? Seriously!" he would complain, half-joking but with a tinge of frustration. Sometimes he just wanted to enjoy a quiet movie night or spend a lazy Sunday without any plans, but with Cintia's regular visits to her mom, it often seemed impossible.

While Cintia was out, Beto decided to take advantage of the free time and went for a run in the park. After finishing his workout, he paused at the public fountain to refill his water bottle. As he did, he casually checked his phone. To his surprise, there were no missed calls or messages—not even from work. What could Cintia be up to? She usually sent him several messages throughout the day, keeping him updated on her activities. The silence felt oddly unsettling.

Beto sat down on a bench, letting the world around him unfold in a peaceful rhythm. He watched as people walked their dogs, children laughed and played with their parents, athletes trained with focused determination, and couples in love cycled together, side by side. The park had always been a refuge for him—a place to unwind, to let his thoughts drift. He appreciated the simplicity of it all, a contrast to the hectic pace of his usual routine. It was moments like these that made him realize how much he enjoyed the quiet and stillness, even if just for a little while.

He picked up his phone again. Nothing. He opened apps, social media, and scrolled through them... Nothing caught his attention. He was alone this weekend; what could he do to distract himself?

Opening his contacts, he stopped at the A section and stared at Aline's name for a while. Should he call her? They had been conversing frequently, collaborating on a work project. Although she was from a different department, she would need Beto's help over the next few months to develop a report. Their initially professional and formal relationship had begun to evolve into something more personal—perhaps too personal. Beto wasn't sure, but he suspected occasional flirtation from her.

"Hello? Beto?" Aline answered promptly.

"I was just thinking... Do you have plans for tonight?"

"Actually, I don't! What are we doing?" she responded, her tone decisive.

"Dinner. At my place, at nine. Do you like wine?"

"Of course. What woman doesn't?"

* * * * *

Beto didn't cook often, but when he did, he was meticulous. He prepared roast beef with vegetables and bought a pie for dessert. For the occasion, he carefully selected the best wine from his small cellar. While he didn't know much about wine, he knew enough to impress.

His apartment was impeccably organized, with light-colored furniture contrasting against dark, mostly black decor. Everything was modern and minimalist. He turned on a soft lamp, casting a warm, romantic glow across the room.

The doorbell rang. Aline stood at the door. Her hair was styled in voluminous waves, and her bright red lipstick made a bold statement. It was clear she'd made an effort to be as sexy as possible. She usually attracted attention naturally, but for this evening, she had prepared from head to toe. She wore a tight dress with a flattering neckline and a pair of elegant, expensive shoes that gave her confidence and made her feel powerful. Aline was bold and assertive—traits that didn't always make her popular among her coworkers.

She politely waited for Beto to invite her in. Once inside, she sat on the couch, waiting to be served. Beto handed her a glass of wine; they toasted and took a sip. The atmosphere was charged, and the exchange of glances between them was intense.

They began dinner discussing work—reports, graphs, and employee reward systems. Aline was surprised when Frank Sinatra started playing on Beto's sound system. They had dessert while sitting on the couch in the living room.

"Did you like the pie?" Beto asked.

"I love it. Walnut is my husband's favorite flavor."

Beto didn't know how to respond. He hadn't noticed a ring, and she had never mentioned being married. Still, he kept his composure, choosing to ignore that "small detail."

Aline sat across from Beto on the same couch. Suddenly, she set her plate on the coffee table, grabbed him by the collar, and kissed him. He didn't hesitate. He kissed her back, reasoning that if anyone should be worried about the marriage, it was her, not him. If she was giving the green light, who was he to question it?

# Twenty-One

Tadeu arrived home and, as usual, pressed his ear against the door. No voices, no sounds—no one was home. He could slip in quietly. The stories Odete had told him were still swirling in his mind, not yet fully processed. He needed to talk to people who knew his father, to find out if the old woman wasn't just making things up. She had said things that only fueled his imagination, especially given everything that had been happening recently.

Then he remembered that day months ago, when he had been at the bar with Beto and Cintia. A drunk had approached him, talking about his father. Yes! He remembered it clearly now. The drunk had even joked that he "wasn't yet like his father", or something along those lines.

Tadeu didn't hesitate. He moved quickly through the streets, his strides long and purposeful. As he entered the bar, he scanned the room, searching for the owner. He spotted an old man, he was unkempt, his face weathered from years in the sun. It didn't take long before the man emerged from a door in the back, struggling under the weight of heavy boxes, which he dropped to the ground with a thud.

"Excuse me, you're the owner here, right?" Tadeu asked.

"Yeah. What do you want?" the old man replied gruffly, one hand resting on his waist.

"I need to talk. My name's Tadeu, and..."

"I know who you are. Walmir's son," the old man interrupted rudely, still chewing on a toothpick hanging from the corner of his mouth.

"Please, this won't take long. Can we sit down for a minute?"

They sat at one of the empty iron tables. Tadeu poured two pints from the pitcher of beer that the old man had brought over.

"Some time ago, I was here with two friends, and a drunk guy approached me. Big guy, shirt wide open, wearing a gold crucifix around his neck. I think he knew my father."

"I know who that guy is," the old man said, pointing toward the sidewalk. "You had a bit of a scene right over there, didn't you? That guy's trouble, picks fights with everyone. But yeah, he and your father used to come here a lot after work, they spent hours playing pool."

"Could you tell me where he lives? I really need to talk to him, please," Tadeu asked.

"What do you want with him? I don't want the police showing up here, making me say things I don't know. You're not planning to do something to him, are you?"

Tadeu let out a tired sigh. "Of course not. I just need to ask some questions to people who knew my father back in the day."

Still suspicious, the old man hesitated before scribbling the drunk guy's address on a worn napkin and handing it to Tadeu.

"I don't want any trouble coming my way, boy," he said, closing the conversation.

* * * * *

Tadeu walked a few blocks and soon found the house listed on the napkin. The street was filthy. Many former employees of a recently-closed factory lived on this block. Most families had lost their main source of income and were scraping by however they could. The houses were rundown and neglected, walls covered in graffiti, yards piled with heaps of garbage, and a general sense of decay hanging over the neighborhood.

Tadeu scanned the area and spotted the number he was looking for. To his surprise, the drunk man was there, sitting in front of the house, surrounded by piles of junk: broken furniture, pieces of wood, old toys—perhaps once belonging to his children—forming an arsenal of debris.

"Can I help you?" the man asked, looking Tadeu up and down. He recognized him but made a point not to show it.

"I know you were a friend of my father's. I'd like to ask you a few quick questions, if that's okay," Tadeu said.

"What do you want to know?" The man gestured for Tadeu to come closer. Amidst the mess, he had to watch where he stepped.

"I'd like to know about the time when my father started going mad, as people say. Can you tell me what happened?"

"Can't say for sure what happened, kid. I just know what your dad used to tell me. I ain't no doctor, so don't go askin' me for no diagnosis or nothin'." Patiently, Tadeu continued with his questions, standing before the man, who still hadn't offered him a seat.

"And what did he used to tell you?"

"It all started when he caught your stepmother—well, your mother, whatever you call her—messin' around with some guy. He just lost it. Said he got home and saw a man slippin' out the kitchen door, headin' for the backyard. When he asked her who it was, she just stood there, bold as anything, sayin' there was no one. Can you believe that? A married woman oughta have some shame. I told your dad he should've left her right then. That woman didn't deserve half of what Walmir did for her." "And why didn't he want to divorce her?"

"Because he said he needed someone to take care of you. At least she knew how to do that well; she stayed with you all day and didn't give your dad any headaches."

"I can't imagine Márcia doing that kind of thing with my dad. It's very strange."

"Well, I didn't know her, but your dad assured me he saw a man inside the house. And it wasn't just once, it happened several times. After a while, he started drinking a lot—that was his way of coping with the problems."

"It's a great way indeed," Tadeu replied, full of irony.

The man scratched his belly with his hairy hand, then wiped his oily forehead. He shifted in his chair and asked, "Is there anything else you want to know?"

"No, I don't think so. Thank you for your time."

As Tadeu turned to leave, he came face-to-face with a woman entering the garden, her arms full of grocery bags. She looked him up and down, slightly surprised.

"Are you Walmir's son? What are you doing here?"

"I'm sorry, ma'am. And you are...?"

"You can call me Tereza. I live in this house. I'm married to that scoundrel sitting next to you, incapable of helping me with the shopping."

The man shrugged, pretending the comment wasn't about him.

"I'm sorry about that. Let me help you." Tadeu reached out his hands toward Tereza, who skeptically handed him two heavy bags. She took the lead and headed toward the front door, with Tadeu following closely behind.

"What did you come to talk to my husband about?" she asked.

"Nothing much, just a few questions about my father."

"Hm... What are you looking for?"

"The truth." For some reason, Tadeu felt comfortable talking to this woman he couldn't remember ever having seen before. "I wasn't very close to my father. I just want to understand these stories about him mistreating my stepmother."

Tereza opened the bags and arranged the items on the table, clearly favoring the cheaper brands. While putting a bag of rice away in the kitchen cabinet, she replied, "I've heard that story before. The few times I ran into Márcia at the market or the fair, she was always very friendly to me. I also saw her at church, dressed so modestly; it's hard to believe she was really bringing men into the house."

"And do you believe she was?" Tadeu asked.

"I don't know. They say Walmir even caught men inside the house. But the truth is, this town is very small, so it's strange that no one ever knew who these men were. I heard your father even tried to track them down; one day he searched the whole neighborhood looking for one of them, but never found anyone."

This was a point that no one had considered so far. In a town where everyone knew each other and meddled in everyone else's business, how had no one ever discovered who these men were? It seemed unlikely.

Tadeu became increasingly convinced of what had happened in the house. He said goodbye to Tereza, thanking her for her time, then crossed the filthy garden, deliberately avoiding the chubby man slumped in the chair.

During the journey home, he reflected deeply on what he had just heard and the people he had just met. That filthy man sitting in the garden, indifferent to helping his wife—of course, Walmir would never have confided in someone like that. Probably, all the men his father had associated with were similar: ignorant individuals who wouldn't understand if he claimed to be seeing things. Walmir likely believed he was being betrayed until he realized that the people he saw weren't real. But by then, the damage was done; he had already begun drinking and becoming violent.

A path of no return.

# Twenty-Two

Cintia was preparing soup for her mother, who was already feeling much better. She sat beside her on the bed, carrying the food on a tray.

"Thank you, dear."

"You don't need to thank me, Mom. How are you feeling?"

"Much better. You can go back home; don't worry about me. I'll be fine."

As Beatriz ate slowly, Cintia sent a message to Beto, explaining that she hadn't been in touch earlier because she had been busy taking care of her mother. She chose not to mention her long conversation with Tadeu; she wasn't sure if Beto would be jealous. Holding her phone in her hands, she waited for a response that never came. Although she trusted her boyfriend, she found everything very strange.

She tried to mentally recall the plans Beto had for the weekend. Could he have gone out for a run? But he never ran at this time. Was he taking a shower? Cooking?

She still carried painful memories of her ex-boyfriend's betrayal, but she didn't want to burden Beto with that; he didn't deserve it.

* * * * *

Cintia drove back to the capital, her gaze fixed on the winding road, surrounded by lush pine trees and numerous farms. It was a two-hour drive through the middle of nowhere. She thought about Beto and his long delay in responding to her messages. He claimed he had gone out to handle some things and had forgotten his phone at home. Should Cintia believe that? Yes, she should. After all, she was starting to feel paranoid again, and that wasn't good. How could she hope to move any relationship forward if she couldn't let go of traumas from years past? She gripped the steering wheel tightly.

Beatriz was unaware of her daughter's suffering. For instance, while single, Cintia often told her mother she was very happy, but the truth was that she had been rejected a few times due to her jealous nature. Two guys she almost started dating backed out because they couldn't handle her possessive ways. Of course, Cintia had never shared this version of the story with anyone. She preferred to present herself as always doing well.

Before meeting Beto shortly, she needed to ensure that her face showed no signs of worry. She forced a smile, glanced in the rearview mirror, and repeated aloud, "It's okay, everything will be fine."

# Twenty-Three

The week began with a rare sun shining in the sky, the temperature pleasantly mild. From the street, the aroma of lunch prepared by Ivone wafted through the air. Max ran back and forth in the garden, playing with his tennis ball, while Odete, as usual, watched everything from her window.

Tadeu had spent the day working, trying to forget recent events. He sent a message to Beto, asking when he would be back in town. The reply came: "In two weeks, maybe. I'm not sure yet."

Determined to get out more, Tadeu decided to look for activities in nearby towns. He needed to meet new people and forget Cintia for good. Flipping through the local newspaper, he noted some upcoming events: there was going to be a fair in a park in a nearby city. He could take Max; it had been a while since he had given the dog any attention.

He arrived home late in the afternoon and petted Max, who jumped with joy as always. Pressing his ear against the door, he didn't hear anyone inside. He entered, unconcerned.

While taking a shower, he heard noises coming from the living room. He already had an idea of what it was about. But... right at shower time? Seriously? He turned off the water and leaned his ear against the door. Two voices. It sounded like the other Tadeu and the other Beto. The other Tadeu spoke loudly:

"Depending on how much I can make from this last delivery, I'll have accumulated a good amount of money. Then I'll be able to move to the capital with Cintia."

"Are you crazy, man? Aren't you risking too much?"

"It's all good. I just need to transport a shipment coming from the border to the capital. I'll drive there, pick up the agreed amount, make the delivery to the address they give me, and that's it."

"You know I never really agreed with what you do, and I hope you stop someday. I can arrange a job for you at the company where I work. What do you think? It won't be much at first, but you can grow from there."

Tadeu wasn't stupid; he was familiar with this conversation and understood exactly what the other Tadeu was talking about. He was definitely transporting drugs for someone. There was no way to know who had requested the job or how much he would be paid, but given the lifestyle he had been leading, the amounts received were likely significant.

From what he could gather, this wasn't the other Tadeu's main occupation; he seemed to have a formal job on the side.

Tadeu remained silent, huddled next to the door, listening carefully to catch any more important information. Suddenly, the doorbell rang; an unidentified third person was at the door.

"Come on in," said the other Tadeu, inviting him inside.

"Hey, man, what's up?" It was a new voice that Tadeu couldn't identify—a young male voice. He heard the other Beto saying goodbye to both of them, leaving, and closing the door.

"So, how's it going?" asked the other Tadeu as he opened a beer and offered it to the third man.

"I need the order delivered next week. I'll give you the address on a piece of paper. Then, the following week, I'll ask you for three more to different cities beyond the border."

"Next week is fine, but I can't do the other orders. I can arrange for someone else to handle them. I won't risk going beyond the border."

"You'll deliver where I tell you to, understand? People are pressuring me hard; I can't involve a stranger at this point in the game." The voice wasn't as friendly as before.

"It's not a 'stranger,' it's someone I trust. I'm moving to another city, and you guys can continue working with him."

Now Tadeu squinted through the keyhole, trying to see what was happening. He could make out the somewhat blurry silhouettes of the two men facing each other, the atmosphere growing tense. His head was throbbing.

"Tadeu, I don't want to have to repeat myself," the other man said, pulling a gun from his waist and spinning it between his fingers. "If I get screwed, you know you're going down with me."

Tadeu felt his stomach turn to ice, his heart racing as if it were about to leap out of his mouth. He covered his lips with his hand, an involuntary gesture of surprise and fear. His eyes widened in shock. He recognized that man; he was much younger than Tadeu and from an influential family in the city.

That was Pedro, Cintia's cousin!

Tadeu had sold drugs to him years ago, back when Pedro was just a playboy trying to impress his friends and the women around him. When he heard Cintia recount the story, he hadn't connected the name to the person. After all, during that time, he supplied drugs to a good portion of the kids in the city and barely remembered most of their names.

It was around the same time that he had trouble with the police. The police chief, accompanied by his subordinates, arrived at his house with a warrant and searched everything. Fortunately, they only found a small amount of drugs, which he claimed were for personal use, along with some stolen items. He managed to get out after a few days and waited for the investigation to commence, but ultimately, the situation led to nothing. Apparently, the other Pedro hadn't abandoned his wild lifestyle either; in fact, he had been profiting from it.

"Man," the other Tadeu raised his hands in a plea. "I want to move to the capital with Cintia. I don't want to do this anymore. If she finds out... she won't forgive me. Please, man, leave me out of this."

"Cintia will understand. After all, what woman doesn't appreciate expensive gifts, like the ones you give her?"

"I'm in love, and I just want to be at peace with her, man. You should want her happiness, too!"

"Of course I do, brother. But a deal is a deal. You promised me you would do this last job. So I'm telling you that the last job will be in installments; I'll want several deliveries on different days."

The other Tadeu scratched his neck, contemplating how to escape the situation. He didn't want to risk driving a car loaded with drugs across the border. If he got caught, he'd be finished. He already had a police record, and the thought of Cintia finding out weighed heavily on him. On top of that, there was the risk of being extorted by corrupt police officers, who often demanded exorbitant amounts to release the "package". He didn't want to lose everything.

Max began scratching at the door, desperate to get inside. The two men exchanged glances—the noise was irritating the other Pedro.

"What the hell is that?"

Seizing the distraction, the other Tadeu acted quickly. In a matter of seconds, he swung the beer bottle he was holding and struck the other Pedro squarely on the head.

The man collapsed, blood pooling on the floor as shards of glass scattered around him.

# Twenty-Four

The other Tadeu stared at the fallen man, realizing that Pedro wasn't unconscious—he was moving slowly, clearly disoriented. Panic surged within him as he scanned the room, desperate for a heavier object to ensure that Pedro wouldn't get up again.

His gaze landed on the coffee table, where a souvenir he had bought with Cintia during a weekend at a farm hotel sat: a stone statuette, a miniature figurehead renowned in the local culture. About fifteen centimeters tall and surprisingly heavy, it seemed to offer the solution he needed.

With grim determination, the other Tadeu struck Pedro's head once, then again, and again. Blood splattered across the sofa, the carpet, and onto his own face. The other Pedro lay motionless on the living room floor—dead, in the shared space of both Tadeus.

Nervous, the other Tadeu could barely breathe; he needed to dispose of the body as quickly as possible. Every second felt like an eternity.

Meanwhile, Tadeu remained in the bathroom, paralyzed by disbelief. He had witnessed the entire scene, feeling suffocated by the horror of it all. Pressing his hands over his ears and closing his eyes tightly, he wished for everything to end. He didn't want to know how the other Tadeu planned to resolve the situation; he just wanted him to vanish so he could escape.

His only desire was to leave and never come back. That house held nothing but bad memories, and he couldn't stand the thought of living there any longer. It felt like a prison, each room echoing with reminders of a life he wanted to forget.

He looked through the keyhole again and saw no one. Silence. Taking a deep breath, he gathered his courage and opened the door. Everything appeared normal; his living room had returned to being just that—his living room. He felt dizzy and nauseous, but he pressed on, opening the wardrobe and yanking out clothes. He tossed everything haphazardly into the suitcase, trembling so much that he couldn't even fold the shirts properly.

But was he really going to leave without telling anyone? Simply disappear? He didn't know, but he couldn't make that decision now. The important thing was to get out of there; he would think about the rest later.

His savings were slim. Would he be able to survive until he sold the house? His thoughts raced, chaotic and frantic, and several times he felt on the verge of fainting.

Then he heard the front door creak open, followed by it slamming shut with the force of the wind. He turned around, his heart pounding, and came face-to-face with the other Tadeu standing in his living room.

They looked at each other from head to toe, the tension palpable. For the first time, an interaction unfolded—bizarre and surreal.

"Who are you? And what are you doing in my house?" the other Tadeu demanded.

"I'm Tadeu. I live here. I'm the owner of this place."

The other Tadeu sank onto the sofa, stunned, his hands pressing against his temples. Desperate, he began to murmur, "This can't be happening. I didn't sign up for this. It's all gone wrong... so wrong."

He glanced around the room, as if searching for an escape, but found only the haunting familiarity of his own home.

"What is this? Am I going crazy? Leave me alone! Leave me alone!"

He squeezed his eyes shut, hoping that, when he opened them, the man who looked exactly like him would vanish.

But he was still there, standing and staring.

Tadeu broke the silence. "I live here, too, just like you. I don't know what's happening or how all this started, but I've been watching you for a long time. Not all the time, but at certain moments of the day—sometimes just seconds, sometimes entire minutes. I realized that our lives are very similar, except you seem to have done better than I have."

He took a step closer, his voice low. "What do we do now?"

"Then it must have been you," the other Tadeu continued. "The things out of place, the unexplained noises, the voices... I thought I was going crazy. To tell the truth, I must be; after all, I'm sitting in my living room, talking to myself. I knew I would end up like my father."

"It might be my madness, too," Tadeu replied, his voice urgent. "But I really need to ask you something... What did you do with Pedro?"

The other Tadeu's eyes widened. He realized he had a witness, and that was the last thing he needed today. What a mess!

"It doesn't matter," he snapped. "What matters is that no one will find him."

Tadeu felt a knot tighten in his stomach. It wasn't just the recent murder that weighed on him; there was something else troubling him deeply. "What if someone does find out? What then?"

"Do you know Odete, who lives across the street?" Tadeu asked.

"What kind of question is that?" the other Tadeu replied, sounding puzzled. "I know her; she's a rude old lady who never treated anyone well."

"I hate to inform you, but she's also incredibly nosy," Tadeu continued, trying to guide his doppelgänger. "She sits by the window all day and knows everyone's routine on this street."

The two men exchanged glances at the window. Fortunately, the curtain was closed. Even if Odete was watching, she would only see people coming and going, with no way to prove anything more than that.

Phew. What a relief.

But the relief was fleeting. Both Tadeus, now terrified, faced a situation they had to resolve together.

# Twenty-Five

The other Tadeu sighed, feeling exhausted. He sank into the sofa, waiting. Wasn't this stranger planning to leave his house? What a situation—what madness.

When he reached the capital, he would see a doctor. If necessary, he would take several prescription medications to find peace. He hoped this entire ordeal would fade into a bad memory from a troubled time.

"The other day, I heard you say you were going to live with Cintia?" Tadeu asked, seizing this rare opportunity to engage with his "more successful" counterpart.

"Yes, why?" the other Tadeu replied.

"Because... here in my life, she's not my girlfriend. She's dating Beto."

"What do you mean? There, where you live, you're not the only one?" The other Tadeu seemed taken aback by this revelation.

"No, there's Cintia, Beto, you—everything is almost exactly the same. Well, not exactly the same; some things differ, but overall, it's very similar."

"That's not possible." The other Tadeu was beginning to realize that his madness was far more intricate than he had initially thought.

"Yes, it is possible. But in both there and here, only you and I seem to notice this happening." Tadeu paused, glancing toward the kitchen. "One day, I was having breakfast right there "He pointed to the table. "And your Cintia saw me while you were asleep in the bedroom. It was the only time."

The other Tadeu stared at him, disbelief etched on his face. The idea that Cintia had seen another version of himself was too surreal to accept. Yet, deep down, he knew that nothing about this situation made sense anymore.

"So, she saw you... and didn't say anything?" he asked, his voice wavering.

"She was confused, but I think she convinced herself it was a dream. After that, everything went back to normal for her."

"Yes... it's true!" The other Tadeu's face lit up as he recalled the incident from some time ago. "I remember her shock, but I thought it was some kind of optical illusion. She really was bewildered."

The two stood there, unable to fully grasp the strange reality they were living. Yet now, with more composure, they began to communicate. The other Tadeu, however, became particularly intrigued by one detail—Cintia dating Beto in the other world.

"So," Tadeu began to explain, "this woman, Aline, the one Beto is dating here." He gestured to the ground, trying to clarify the separation of realities. "She's not with him there. Cintia fell in love with him, and they're together."

The other Tadeu furrowed his brow, trying to make sense of it all. "But how? How could she fall for him there when she's with me here?"

Tadeu shrugged. "I don't know. It just happened. Maybe it's the same way you and she ended up together here."

The other Tadeu stood frozen, staring at his phone after the call with Cintia. The revelation of her relationship with Beto in the other world gnawed at him. He had always believed in her love, but now, for the first time, a seed of jealousy had been planted. Dating Beto? The thought alone made his chest tighten.

As he lowered his phone, he turned to look for the other Tadeu, but the room was empty. His heart raced as he scanned the space. No trace of him remained. Only silence.

The weight of the situation pressed down on him. Was it all a dream? Had he imagined everything? But the lingering feeling of unease, the jealousy, and the eerie calmness in the room told him otherwise.

He was alone, but the reality of what had just transpired lingered like a shadow.

# Twenty-Six

Tadeu sat up, his heart racing as he tried to process everything. The room looked the same as before, but it felt different now, as though it carried the weight of all that had happened. He rubbed his temples, hoping to make sense of the chaos. *Did I really see all that? Did I really talk to him?*

His mind wandered back to the conversation with the other Tadeu, the bizarre reflection of himself who seemed to have taken a darker path in life. He had never imagined himself capable of committing a crime—well, not *that* kind of crime. Killing someone is on a whole different level. It's not the same as selling drugs, is it? Yet the other Tadeu had done it so easily, with the calm precision of someone who had done it before. It left a sour feeling in his gut.

He wondered what had led the other Tadeu down that road. Was it just circumstance, or had something deeper inside him—inside both of them—always been there, waiting to surface? The thought chilled him. What if, under the right conditions, he, too, could become that version of himself?

Tadeu stood and paced around the living room. He couldn't stay here much longer. This place, once his sanctuary, now felt haunted by his other self and by the memory of Pedro's murder. He needed to get away, to escape the oppressive feeling that had settled over him since this strange parallel life had entered his own.

But where would he go? And what would he do about Cintia? If the other Tadeu was planning a future with her, what did that mean for him? Was he destined to lose her to this twisted version of his life?

The questions swirled in his head as he glanced at the front door. For the first time in a long while, the idea of leaving everything behind didn't seem so far-fetched.

The thought was faint at first, almost laughable in its absurdity. But the more Tadeu turned it over in his mind, the more it began to take shape, creeping into the corners of his consciousness until it became impossible to ignore.

*What if I could switch lives with him?*

He shook his head, trying to dismiss the notion. It was madness, but wasn't everything about this situation already insane? He envied the other Tadeu's boldness—the confidence with which he lived, even if it was rooted in danger and crime. He'd been miserable in his own life for so long that even the absurd situation he had just witnessed seemed better than reality. His obsession with having Cintia had only grown.

Lately, so much had been bubbling to the surface, especially the unresolved questions about his past and his family. It was something he should've faced a long time ago. He felt so incompetent, he hadn't even managed to do that much for himself. He had been living an inert life, aimless, passive, sad. It had taken this madness to finally push him into action. How pathetic was that?

Reconnecting with Beto after all this time had felt like a sign, a reminder that a new beginning was still possible. It was the slap in the face he had needed.

Despite the risks, the other Tadeu had something Tadeu had never managed to claim for himself: control, or at least the illusion of it. He took what he wanted, while Tadeu had spent years stuck in hesitation, constantly fearful of judgment, failure, or simply being too much of a coward to go after what he desired.

*If I had his life,* he thought, *I'd have Cintia. I'd have the confidence to be with her. Maybe I'd even have the guts to be a real man, instead of the indecisive mess I've always been.*

Tadeu paced, feeling the weight of the idea grow heavier. The more he imagined the possibilities, the less absurd it seemed. The other Tadeu had already committed murder, already crossed lines he could never even imagine approaching. But if they were so alike— two halves of the same life, somehow split—why couldn't he step into the shoes of the other Tadeu and live that bold, daring life?

*What's stopping me?*

# Twenty-Seven

The other Tadeu's thoughts raced, the weight of his actions pressing heavily on him. He couldn't afford a single misstep. His mind kept replaying the scene with Pedro, over and over, and every time, the fear gnawed at him—what if someone found out? What if they were already suspicious?

He continued scratching his neck, an anxious habit he couldn't seem to shake. He had to keep calm, keep his story straight. *But which story?* he thought bitterly. Every possible scenario he imagined brought a different set of complications. If he said he didn't know Pedro, it might raise suspicion—too many people knew of their connection. But admitting Pedro had been there was risky, too. What if someone had seen them together? Odete? Someone else? His heart skipped at the thought.

*I need to be smart about this,* he told himself. *Simple. Clean. No loose ends.*

He decided on his version of events: yes, Pedro had come by. Yes, they'd had a brief conversation, but Pedro had left soon after. He had no idea where Pedro had gone or what had happened after. It was plausible, enough to throw off any suspicion. He would act normal, keep to his routine, and make sure no one had any reason to doubt him. The key was confidence—he had to convince himself first before he could convince anyone else.

But underneath the careful planning, a nagging fear lingered. What if Tadeu—the other Tadeu—had seen everything? Would he stay silent, or would he use this knowledge against him?

He sat back, rubbing his hands together, trying to calm his nerves. For now, he had to wait, and waiting was the hardest part.

The other Tadeu sat in silence, wrestling with the weight of what lay ahead.

Pedro came from an influential family, with money, status, and connections—everything most people lacked. Still, he had ended up in drug trafficking, a choice that seemed senseless given his background. Whatever had driven him to that path no longer mattered. That chapter was already closed.

Cintia would eventually hear about Pedro's disappearance, and when she did, it would hit her hard. She had always been close to her family, even if she hadn't seen them much in person lately, life, work, and everything in between just kept getting in the way. She and Pedro had grown up together, along with his sister. The pain would ripple through her family, and Tadeu would have to stand there, listen to her heartbreak, and pretend he knew nothing. He could already picture the endless conversations, the worry, the sorrow, the accusations, none of which could truly reach him. He would have to play his part perfectly, suppressing any sign of guilt or knowledge. No one could ever know. He'd have to nod along, offer support, maybe even fake concern. At this point, he had no other choice.

* * * * *

In the river that wound its way along the trail to the old abandoned power plant, a body lay hidden, slowly decomposing inside a black garbage bag, weighed down by a pile of rocks. The water, usually so clear and serene, was now part of a dark secret, masking the decay beneath its surface.

It was an eerie coincidence, or perhaps fate, that this very spot had once been where Beto and Tadeu camped as kids. Back then, the river had been a place of carefree adventures, where they'd spend summer afternoons fishing and telling ghost stories by the fire. Now the same place bore the weight of a horrifying truth, a stark reminder of how far their lives had diverged from those innocent days.

# Twenty-Eight

Cintia rang the doorbell of Beto's apartment, still without a set of keys. "One step at a time," he always told her. When Beto opened the door, they embraced, and Cintia whispered how much she had missed him during her time away caring for her mother. He smiled, kissed her softly, and welcomed her inside. The apartment was, as usual, impeccably tidy. Beto was meticulous, never one for clutter or chaos. But tonight, there was another reason for the orderliness—he couldn't let Cintia suspect that anyone else had been there.

They spent the evening together, their routine easy and comfortable. They rented a movie online, ordered takeout, and curled up on the couch. After dinner, they made love. Beto drifted into a deep sleep, but Cintia remained awake. Lying beside him in the double bed, she stared at the ceiling, her thoughts racing. Insomnia clung to her, amplifying the unease that had been gnawing at her since her trip.

Something had changed. Beto's delayed responses when she was away had been eating at her, making her feel uncertain. Though she tried to push the thoughts aside, they screamed louder in the silence of the night.

Cintia went to the bathroom, splashing cold water on her face before looking at herself in the mirror. She was undeniably beautiful, yet a sense of insecurity gnawed at her. Her mind raced, making sleep impossible at that hour. Her sixth sense nagged at her, whispering that something wasn't right.

Quietly, she tiptoed back into the bedroom, feeling the chill from the air conditioning seep into her bones. She moved carefully, determined not to wake Beto. As she felt around in the dark, her fingers brushed against his bedside table and found his phone. Heart racing, she returned to the bathroom with the device in hand. She had seen him enter the code to unlock the screen earlier.

Should she snoop? Her heart urged her on, while her rational mind cautioned against it. It felt like a battle was raging within her, a devil on one shoulder and an angel on the other, each vying for dominance in her dilemma. The tension in her chest grew, and she hesitated, torn between curiosity and the trust she wanted to uphold. It took her several minutes to make the decision. Finally, unable to resist the urge, she unlocked the device.

Messages flooded the screen, revealing all the exchanges between Beto and Aline. None explicitly crossed any lines, but the tone felt far too intimate for two coworkers merely collaborating on a report. Flirty banter mixed with personal anecdotes painted a picture of a connection that seemed to surpass professional boundaries. Cintia's heart sank as she scrolled through, a sense of unease settling over her like a heavy blanket. Doubts crept in, and the insecurities that had plagued her began to swell. How well did she really know Beto? She sat on the toilet and began to cry, disbelief washing over her as she confronted the emotional turmoil yet again. Fear, insecurity, jealousy—these feelings surged back like a turbulent wave on a stormy sea, threatening to pull her under. Cintia felt on the brink of losing control, desperately trying to hold it together.

Wiping her face and combing her hair, she glanced at her reflection in the mirror. "It's okay, it will be okay," she whispered to herself, searching for reassurance in her own eyes. Yet deep down, she knew she couldn't share her struggles with anyone. Cintia had always been the strong one, masking her pain behind a facade of strength. She would carry this burden alone, keeping the facade intact.

# Twenty-Nine

Cintia had convinced Beto to spend the weekend with her in the countryside. She wanted to check on Beatriz and didn't want Beto to be alone in the city; her discomfort about his solitude nagged at her. When Beto got into the car, he was silent, clearly unhappy. He asked her to drop him off at his mother's house, expressing disinterest in visiting his future mother-in-law. She agreed, though she felt a twinge of disappointment; she wished Beto would show more interest in her family.

As they arrived, Ivone was in the garden, finishing up by pulling out some dead flowers. She liked to keep it looking nice. She was wearing a straw hat and gardening gloves, along with a light summer dress., she resembled a peasant woman, bustling about with her tools and watering can. Max kept her company, having recently taken to spending more time with her than with his own owner.

Beto helped his mother gather the dry leaves scattered across the yard, and soon the lawn looked as beautiful as it should. Ivone then began to ask questions about her son's relationship, but she had to settle for short and shallow answers, which frustrated her. She longed for her son to be more enthusiastic about his life and the love therein.

Afterward, Beto headed over to Tadeu's house, opening the door that was always left unlocked. He grabbed a beer from the fridge and took a seat at the kitchen table. Tadeu had sent a message letting him know he was on his way.

When Tadeu finally arrived, Beto immediately noticed that his friend looked worn out. He had lost weight and hadn't shaved, making him appear disheveled.

"What truck ran over you, man?" Beto asked, concern etched on his face.

"None, just been really busy lately," Tadeu replied, looking a bit embarrassed.

"Come on, I'll treat you to lunch."

"What about your mom? Won't she be upset if you skip lunch with her?" Tadeu inquired, raising an eyebrow.

"No, she's having lunch with the church folks. So we can all have dinner together tonight."

They walked along the wet sidewalks and arrived at a bakery that offered a lunch buffet. Tadeu wasn't very hungry, so he filled his plate sparingly and ordered a beer. He had been drinking too much lately, using it as an escape from the chaos that had taken over his life. He feared ending up like his father, but by the third can, he cared less about that.

The two talked about everything: work, routines, money—or the lack thereof.

★ ★ ★ ★ ★

Cintia had finished washing the dishes and organizing the kitchen before sitting down to keep Beatriz, who was watching a soap opera, company. Cintia's eyes were also fixed on the screen, but she wasn't really paying attention to what was being broadcast, because a name kept hammering in her head: Aline.

She placed her hand on her mother's landline phone, wondering if she should call Aline's number, which she had already memorized. She wouldn't be foolish enough to call from her own cell phone, of course, as Beto would quickly find out. She took a deep breath— one, two, three times—but the urge didn't pass; her sixth sense kept begging her to investigate the situation.

She dialed the number she had memorized. The phone rang. It took a moment, but a voice answered on the other end.

"Hello."

Cintia had mustered the courage to call but hadn't thought about what she would say. She remained silent. Aline said "hello" three more times. Finally, Cintia spoke up.

"Hello... is this Aline speaking?"

"Yes... Who's calling?"

Cintia quickly scanned the room for something that could provide her with an idea right then and there. On top of a piece of furniture, an old pamphlet from a local farm hotel that had closed down long ago caught her eye. She cleared her throat and took a deep breath. "Well, this is from the Enchantment Farm Hotel. Beto made a reservation with us and left his number in case we couldn't reach him."

Very good.

"I'm calling to confirm your upcoming visit next weekend. We sent an email regarding a last-minute room change due to renovations, but we haven't received a response."

"Reservation? Farm hotel? I have no idea about any of this."

Cintia realized it would be difficult to get the woman to say anything incriminating about the couple. With nothing to lose, she pressed on.

"Did I ruin a surprise? Aline, I apologize for any inconvenience. We'll continue trying to reach him anyway..."

"Wait, what reservation is this? For this weekend?" Aline interrupted, her voice tinged with confusion. She found the situation odd. Beto knew she was married and couldn't just make plans like this. Even if it was a surprise, albeit a romantic one, she couldn't just unexpectedly go to a hotel with her lover.

"Yes, I managed to book you in the best suite with an incredible view of the lake. If you're celebrating something special, you're sure to love it."

"Well, maybe another time. I'll have to ask Beto to cancel the reservation. We won't be able to come this weekend."

"You don't need to worry about that. We'll contact him again. I apologize for any inconvenience, Aline. I hope you can enjoy your stay another time."

Cintia hung up the phone abruptly, not giving the woman on the other end a chance to continue the conversation. She had little time before confronting Beto, before he found out about this story.

Cintia felt her face flush, her heart filled with anger, her hands trembling, and tears choked in her throat. She got up quickly, unable to contain her emotions. Grabbing the car keys, she hastily got into the vehicle without saying goodbye to her mother. She raced to Ivone's house, hoping to find Beto there. She didn't want to call; just from his tone of voice, he would know something was wrong and have time to think of some lame excuse. No! She wanted to catch him by surprise.

Not finding Beto at home, she drove through the city, passing places where she thought he might be. Nervous and not paying attention to where she was going, she discovered he wasn't in the square or at Tadeu's house. It was lunchtime, and then it hit her: the bakery. They served food at that time of day.

★ ★ ★ ★ ★

Tadeu was already on his fourth beer when Cintia burst in, her demeanor frantic and intense. Her eyes were swollen, and her face was flushed with anger. She didn't want to cause a scene by yelling or drawing attention to their table, but her nervousness was palpable. For the first time, she couldn't pretend that everything was okay.

"Beto, let's leave now. We need to talk!"

"What's wrong? Is everything okay with your mom? Did something happen?"

Cintia was extremely irritated. How could he be so cynical? He never asked about her mother, never showed any interest in her life—why this sudden show of concern? Deep down, he obviously knew it wasn't about Beatriz.

"My mom is fine, you son of a bitch!"

Tadeu stood up immediately, sensing the gravity of the situation. He placed his hands on Cintia's shoulders, but she shrugged off the gesture, quickly pulling away.

"Calm down, sweetheart. Let's go outside; you're nervous and—"

"'Sweetheart'? Is that how you talk to her, too?"

At that moment, everyone in the bakery stopped what they were doing to witness the unfolding drama. Beto stood up, pulled out some bills from his wallet, and tossed them onto the table. He grabbed Cintia by the arm and led her out onto the street.

"What are you talking about? Are you crazy?"

"I'm not crazy. I know you and Aline have more than a professional friendship. I don't know how long it's been going on... You didn't sleep with her in our bed, did you?"

"First, calm down." He took a deep breath. "Second, there's nothing between me and her. And third, the bed is mine, not ours." Beto knew how to be infuriating when he wanted to be; what was the point of that last comment?

Tadeu watched everything unfold but remained silent, not wanting to interfere. At the same time, he struggled to contain himself as a small smile threatened to appear at the corner of his mouth. Was this fake relationship finally coming to an end? With Beto out of the way, things would be much easier; he could finally get closer to Cintia, offer her a friendly shoulder, and before she knew it, they would have a good vibe going. He no longer cared about her and Beto's involvement. Beto didn't like her the same way he did.

He wouldn't need to envy the other Tadeu anymore because he would also have a Cintia to call his own.

Beto pulled Cintia away, managing to calm her down and convincing her to go to Ivone's house for a private talk. As they walked, tension hung in the air, thick with unspoken accusations and simmering emotions. Cintia's heart raced, torn between anger and the lingering affection she felt for Beto, while Tadeu watched them go, a mix of hope and anticipation bubbling within him. This could be his chance to finally step into a reality he had long envied.

# Thirty

Tadeu sat on the porch, avoiding the confines of the house. His last encounter with the other Tadeu had left him feeling unsettled, blurring the lines between reality and hallucination. He called for Max, his loyal dog, and together they passed the afternoon in companionable silence, the warmth of the sun casting a comforting glow.

As the hours stretched on, Tadeu felt a growing fatigue. The weight of the house pressed down on him, suffocating and chaotic, contrasting sharply with the normalcy he experienced when he was away. It was a place steeped in madness, echoing the turmoil that had driven his father to the brink. The thought of becoming yet another victim of its oppressive presence gnawed at him. With each passing moment, he yearned to escape its grasp, knowing that the next resident might also fall prey to its haunting shadows.

The money Tadeu had saved wasn't nearly enough for him to leave right away. His only option was to put the property up for sale and endure the waiting game until the transaction was completed. He sighed, a wave of sadness washing over him. Who would want to buy an old house at the end of the world?

* * * * *

Inside the house, the other Tadeu and the other Cintia sat together, tension filling the air. Beatriz had just called Cintia with devastating news: her cousin, Pedro, had gone missing, and the family was in turmoil. Her uncle was inconsolable, his grief palpable even over the phone. The police had already initiated a search, and local newspapers were relentlessly calling the family, eager for any updates on the young man's disappearance.

The weight of the situation loomed heavy in the room as the implications began to sink in. The other Tadeu felt a cold sweat on his brow, torn between the turmoil of his own actions and the reality of the chaos unfolding around him. Cintia's face reflected a mixture of concern and confusion as she processed the information, her thoughts racing to understand how this could have happened.

* * * * *

Tadeu's phone buzzed with a message from Cintia, causing his heart to race. What did she want?

"I'm sorry for the embarrassing situation. Beto and I have sorted things out. I'm really ashamed of how I reacted. I promise not to cause any more discomfort."

It wasn't the kind of message he had been expecting. Tadeu thought she might reach out for a friendly shoulder, someone to confide in. Instead, after reading her words, he was filled with anger. He clenched his fist and punched the wall hard, the pain in his knuckles a mere distraction from the frustration boiling inside him. How could they reconcile so easily? How did Beto always come out on top, never letting Tadeu win—not even once? Of course, Beto wasn't aware that Tadeu had been competing with him for Cintia, because, as always, Tadeu had let the opportunity slip by in silence—and that made him even more furious. Coward. That's what he was. A coward who always blamed others for his failures but never himself.

Fuming, he slammed the door behind him as he entered the house, the sound echoing through the empty rooms. Max whimpered and scurried to hide under the table, sensing the tension radiating from his owner. Tadeu stood there, seething with rage, feeling trapped in a cycle he couldn't escape. Every moment felt like a reminder of his failures, and the anger only fueled his growing desire to break free from the life he found so suffocating.

If it weren't for those infernal hallucinations, Tadeu would have ignored the whole story: him and Cintia dating. But witnessing the other Tadeu and the other Cintia together made him painfully aware of what he was missing—how good it could feel to be with someone, to love and be loved.

He opened the fridge, but beer felt too weak for his current state. His gaze drifted to the back of the cupboard, where a bottle of whiskey sat waiting. Without bothering to grab a glass, he unscrewed the cap and took a long swig straight from the bottle, the burn of the alcohol cutting through the haze of his frustration. The whiskey didn't just numb his anger; it drowned out the memories of what could have been, if only his life hadn't spiraled so far off-course.

As he leaned against the counter, the room began to spin slightly, a familiar haze clouding his thoughts. With each gulp, he tried to forget about the other Tadeu, the other Cintia, and the life that felt so tantalizingly out of reach. Instead, he found himself sinking deeper into a sense of despair, a longing for connection that whiskey couldn't fill.

* * * * *

Beto had invited Tadeu for dinner at his mother's house, but after several failed attempts to reach him by call and text, he decided to stop by Tadeu's place. Ivone had gone all out with the dinner menu, and he didn't want to let her efforts go to waste.

When Beto opened the door, he was startled to find Tadeu collapsed on the floor, drunker than he had ever seen him. A wave of concern washed over him as he rushed inside, quickly assessing the situation. Tadeu's face was pale, and empty whiskey bottles littered the room, a grim testament to his friend's state.

Beto knelt down, carefully lifting Tadeu into his arms. The weight of his friend felt heavier than usual, and he struggled slightly but managed to get him off the floor. He carried Tadeu to his bed, where he gently laid him down, taking off his shoes and coat. After covering him with a warm blanket, Beto turned off the lights, casting the room into a comforting darkness.

"Just sleep it off," Beto murmured, hoping Tadeu would be fine in the morning. He knew he'd wake up with a massive hangover, but at least he wouldn't be alone in this state. Beto quietly exited the room, leaving Tadeu to rest while he contemplated how to help his friend through whatever storm he was facing.

Tadeu eventually woke up to the sound of commotion echoing around him. Still drunk and lacking a filter, he began to hurl accusations at Beto, the words tumbling out in a jumbled mess. His thoughts weren't entirely clear, but he had been harboring these feelings for far too long.

"You're a jerk, man. Why are you still dating Cintia? And who's this Aline? How can you be such a scumbag? Cintia doesn't deserve this."

Beto sighed, rubbing his temples in frustration. "You're wasted, man. Let's talk about this tomorrow." He didn't want to delve into his relationship or justify his choices to anyone, especially not in this state.

"I don't want to talk tomorrow! I want to know now... tell me now, you son of a bitch. Are you having an affair with this Aline? You have a wonderful woman who does absolutely everything for you!" Tadeu's voice cracked with anger and hurt, the words spilling out like a dam that had finally broken.

Beto's patience wore thin as he faced Tadeu's drunken outburst. "This isn't the time or place for this," he replied, his voice steady but firm. "You're not in a good place to have this conversation."

"Why not? Because I'm drunk? Or because you can't handle the truth?" Tadeu shot back, struggling to sit up. His frustration was palpable, fueled by jealousy and a sense of betrayal he couldn't quite articulate.

Beto felt the tension rise, realizing that this confrontation was inevitable. "Just sit down and calm down. We can talk about this when you're sober," he replied, trying to defuse the situation before it escalated further.

Beto didn't need more than that to understand what was happening. Tadeu was hopelessly in love and had stopped bothering to hide it. "As if I needed this," Beto sneered, leaning in slightly. "Tadeu, do you really think she'd be with a guy like you? A guy who's never done anything decent in his life?!"

"I know she wouldn't be with a guy like me!" Tadeu shot back, his voice rising in anger. "And I'm really pissed that she's with a guy like you, and you couldn't care less, you jerk!" He pointed his index finger at Beto, a gesture that was both accusatory and desperate.

Beto took a step back, a mix of surprise and annoyance flickering across his face. "You think I don't care?" he asked incredulously. "You think I'm just some heartless bastard who doesn't appreciate what I have?"

"Yeah, it sure looks that way!" Tadeu retorted, his emotions spilling over. "You're with her, but you're still flirting with that Aline woman. It's like you don't even see how good you have it."

Beto clenched his jaw, feeling the sting of Tadeu's words. "You don't know anything about my relationship with Cintia. You don't see the whole picture," he shot back, frustration bubbling beneath the surface.

"Maybe I don't," Tadeu replied, his voice shaking with intensity. "But I see enough to know that she deserves better than a guy who can't even be honest with her."

Beto felt a surge of irritation, but beneath it lay a flicker of doubt. Could Tadeu be right? In that moment, he realized the weight of the confrontation, and the air grew heavy with unspoken truths and simmering tensions.

"Well, Tadeu, if you want to try, go ahead," Beto taunted, a smirk creeping onto his face. "Take advantage while she's still mad at me; let's see if you can manage it. With a sad past like yours, such a mediocre life... you even have a police record. A woman like Cintia would never even look at you. No woman would want to be with a loser like you."

Tadeu stood there, his heart sinking under the weight of Beto's words. He had nothing to say in response. All those accusations were true. He was a loser, and he didn't deserve Cintia's love—or anyone else's, for that matter. The bitterness of Beto's insult stung deep, a painful reminder of his failures. He was doomed to spend the rest of his life alone, with only Max by his side for company.

"Just remember this," Beto continued, leaning in closer, "while you're busy pining over Cintia, I'm the one who's actually with her. I'm the one who gets to hold her, kiss her, and be in her life. You're just a name she once knew."

Tadeu clenched his fists, trying to hold back the wave of emotions threatening to overflow. "You're right," he finally muttered, his voice low and defeated. "You're the one with her." He turned away, unable to meet Beto's gaze any longer.

For a moment, the room fell silent, the air thick with tension and unspoken resentment. Tadeu knew he needed to walk away before he said something he'd regret, but the ache in his chest made it hard to breathe. He stumbled toward the door, feeling the weight of Beto's laughter echoing in his ears as he stepped out into the night. He stood frozen on the porch, trying to quiet his own thoughts, to make sense of everything he had just heard, the cool air doing little to soothe the fire within. Tadeu would become the new "Odete" of the neighborhood, a reclusive figure shunned by everyone. All the kids would fear him, and he would die alone. After months, they would find his body, a forgotten relic in an abandoned house. His home would become infamous, a ghostly reminder of a life once lived, until the day the city decided to turn that trash into something else.

After a few minutes, he sensed Beto's presence right behind him. "Get out of here, Beto. Leave me alone," Tadeu murmured, his eyes were red, swollen from unshed tears and the alcohol that still coursed through his system. He felt utterly defeated, as if the walls were closing in on him.

Beto huffed, the smugness evaporating from his face. "Fine. But don't say I didn't warn you." He paused, taking one last look at his friend, the weight of their fractured friendship hanging heavily in the air. "Just... think about what I said."

Tadeu didn't respond. Instead, he focused on the dull throb in his head and the creeping sense of despair that had become all too familiar. Beto was furious with Tadeu for meddling in his relationship. He took a few heavy steps toward the exit, the floor echoing under his feet—but just seconds after passing Tadeu, he spun around and confronted him.

"You know what, Tadeu?! You should be thanking me. I'm the one who dragged you out of that shitty life you were living. If no one had stopped you, you'd probably be in jail or dead by now."

"What... What do you mean by that?" Tadeu widened his eyes, shocked.

"That time when the police showed up at your house and took you to the station? I was the one who reported you. I let you stay locked up for a few days to learn what your fate would be. You needed to feel it—just telling you didn't work. How many times did I try to warn you? How many times did we talk about this? Then I talked to the detective, pulled a few strings here and there, and they released you. You know how great the police are here— a bunch of lazy pigs who avoid work. The whole scene didn't cost me much."

Tadeu's mind raced. He felt as if the ground had shifted beneath him. The betrayal cut deeper than any insult.

"You... you reported me? You did that to me?"

In that moment, it felt like any trace of alcohol in Tadeu's blood had evaporated along with his composure. The shock of it sobered him instantly.

"Yeah, I did. And you know what? It was the best thing I could have done for you. You might hate me now, but at least you're not six feet under."

Tadeu's heart pounded in his chest, anger and disbelief swirling within him. "You think you were helping me? You ruined my life!"

Beto crossed his arms, unimpressed. "No, I saved your life. You just don't get it. You were on a self-destructive path, and I had to intervene."

The realization hit Tadeu like a freight train, and he struggled to process the truth behind Beto's words. The tension in the room felt electric, each second stretching into eternity as they locked eyes, each man unwilling to back down.

"I'll never thank you for this," Tadeu finally spat, bitterness lacing his voice. "You had no right to make that decision for me."

"Maybe not, but look at where you are now. You're alive," Beto shot back, his voice hardening.

Tadeu was overwhelmed by the weight of betrayal and shame. He had lost more than just his freedom back then; he had lost his trust in his closest friend.

"I can't believe it. I can't believe you ruined my life," Tadeu said, his voice trembling with rage and disbelief.

"You better believe it. And you should thank me, because if you have any chance with any woman, it's because of me. I turned you into a... somewhat more... let's say, a respectable man."

Tadeu couldn't process the betrayal, especially coming from Beto—his best friend since childhood. Their friendship had been strained lately, that much was true, but he never expected this. It felt like a knife had plunged deep into his back. He was struck by the realization that Beto seemed to relish in his suffering, as if he didn't want him to succeed.

"Just go away, Beto. Leave me alone. I hate you for stealing the life I could have had," Tadeu spat, bitterness flooding his words.

Beto's expression hardened. "Stealing? I saved you from yourself! You were on a path to self-destruction, and I did what I had to do."

"Saved me? Is that what you call it?" Tadeu shot back. "You took away my choice, my freedom. You had no right to play judge and jury over my life!"

"Maybe not, but you were too far gone to see it. You think you could have turned your life around on your own? Look where that got you."

"Look where it got me?" Tadeu echoed, incredulous. "I'm stuck in this hellhole, struggling just to make ends meet, and you act like you're some kind of savior?"

Beto took a step closer, frustration etching his features. "You're blaming me for your problems instead of facing your own mistakes. I tried to help you, Tadeu. I really did."

"Help?" Tadeu laughed bitterly. "You think this is help? You've created a monster out of guilt and obligation. I'll never see you the same way again."

With that, Tadeu turned away, a sense of finality settling between them. Their friendship, once a source of strength, now felt like a chain dragging him down. He couldn't shake the feeling that he would need to leave everything behind—including Beto—if he ever wanted to find his own way.

Beto didn't quite grasp what Tadeu meant by "stealing the life I could have had", but he dismissed it as the incoherent ramblings of a drunk who wasn't thinking straight.

Meanwhile, Tadeu felt a whirlwind of emotions swirling within him. He had become a spectator of his own life over the past few months, watching the other Tadeu—the improved version of himself—thrive. In a different reality, he would be happy, financially secure, and, most importantly, with Cintia. Beto had taken away his only chance to become "someone better".

The thought consumed him. He wished with all his might that Beto would simply disappear from the planet. The desire to erase himself followed closely behind—he felt as though he was being swallowed by despair.

As he wallowed in those dark thoughts, he heard Beto's footsteps retreating, the sound of them growing more distant. His supposed friend was finally leaving, slamming the door behind him. Tadeu was left in a silence that felt oppressive, the weight of betrayal pressing down on him like a heavy blanket.

# Thirty-One

The other Tadeu accompanied the other Cintia to the police station to give a statement, as the sheriff had requested to hear from everyone who had had any contact with Pedro in the past few weeks. Unfortunately, the search for the young man wasn't shaping up to be an easy task. His family had already mentioned that Pedro often failed to provide updates about his life. He didn't have a girlfriend, and the few friends called in to testify couldn't shed any light on his whereabouts.

Moreover, the local police were ill-equipped and underprepared to handle such cases; they were more accustomed to dealing with petty crimes like chicken thefts and cats stuck in trees. Sheriff Antunes, embodying his characteristic lack of enthusiasm, had his feet propped up on the table, lazily perusing the latest reports when he received the grim news that a body had been found floating in the river near the trail by the old abandoned power plant.

The announcement sent a ripple of tension through the small station. Sheriff Antunes straightened up, his eyes narrowing as he processed the implications. He grabbed his hat, an urgent sense of purpose replacing his earlier apathy.

"Let's move," he called out to his deputy, the gravity of the situation finally sinking in. The sheriff knew that in a town like theirs, this was no ordinary event, and it could mean trouble—trouble that the unprepared police force would have to face head on.

Outside, the sun was beginning to set, casting a dim light over the town as they made their way to the river. The air was thick with anticipation and dread; for the families affected, the discovery of Pedro's body could be the closure they dreaded but needed.

He arrived at the scene to find that the body had already been pulled from the river. It was confirmed: it was Pedro. His face was disfigured, apparently from numerous blows, and his body was pale and swollen from spending an extended period in the water.

When the news reached Pedro's family, they were understandably devastated. His mother collapsed upon hearing the tragic news, requiring sedatives to calm her nerves. The story spread throughout the town like wildfire; whispers filled the air as people grappled with the grim reality of the situation, unable to stop talking about it.

The other Tadeu chose to remain silent. He had hidden Pedro's cellphone and gun, certain that if questioned by the police, he could claim that he had never known Pedro intimately. To some extent, he felt a strange sense of calm. The involvement of illegal activities had created an unspoken code among those who knew Pedro, and he was confident that the people connected to him in that world wouldn't dare show their faces for a long time.

As the sheriff and his deputy began their investigation, the weight of secrecy hung heavily in the air. The other Tadeu knew the risks of what he had done, but he also understood the fragile nature of their town—how quickly rumors could morph into truths and how quickly lives could be irrevocably changed. With Pedro's death, the delicate balance that held their lives together had shifted, and he could only hope to remain unseen in the aftermath.

He needed to continue with the lie. If Cintia found out everything, her disappointment would be twofold: first, for never imagining that Tadeu had been involved in drug trafficking, and second, because she could never accept being in a relationship with a murderer, especially her cousin's murderer.

During the investigation, the family requested that the sheriff not allow the media access to the police reports. The manner in which the body had been discovered was already stirring up enough questions and gossip among the townsfolk, creating headaches for everyone involved. The sheriff knew that managing public perception was just as important as finding the truth.

With pressure mounting to show results, Sheriff Antunes spent several days interrogating the residents of the town. However, the responses were frustratingly vague. No one was willing to provide him with useful information, each person preferring to remain silent rather than risk becoming embroiled in the investigation. The tight-knit community had an unspoken understanding about not getting involved in the darker dealings of their neighbors, and fear of repercussions kept many lips sealed.

As days turned into weeks, the sheriff's frustration grew. He felt the weight of responsibility bearing down on him, the cries for justice growing louder with each passing day. He understood that without cooperation from the community, he was fighting an uphill battle against both the criminals and the very people he was sworn to protect. Meanwhile, the other Tadeu moved through the town with a sense of dread, knowing that every interaction could potentially unravel the precarious web of lies he had woven to protect himself. Due to the violent nature of the crime, it was likely that Pedro had known his killer. The severity of the blows suggested that the perpetrator was someone who harbored deep anger toward him. In rivalry situations, it was common for the suspect to vent their rage on the victim with repeated strikes, as if to ensure their death while simultaneously unleashing the adrenaline fueled by hatred.

Now, the sheriff needed to uncover what kind of trouble the boy had been involved in. He couldn't rule out possibilities like a love triangle, gang conflicts, or drug trafficking. Each theory added another layer of complexity to the investigation, making it clear that Pedro's life had been entangled with darker forces.

Getting witnesses to come forward from the community proved challenging; no one wanted to approach the police to discuss Pedro, especially those who were his clients—other children from wealthy, traditional families in the area. They were more concerned about protecting their own reputations than seeking justice for a boy who had been living on the edge.

Suddenly, the sheriff was interrupted by an on-duty officer.

"Sheriff, there's someone who wants to speak with you. They say it's about the Pedro case."

"Send them in," he replied, his curiosity piqued.

As the door opened, a nervous-looking young woman stepped inside. Her eyes darted around the room, revealing her anxiety, but there was a determination in her posture. She had clearly made the decision to come forward, and the sheriff hoped that she held the key to unraveling the tangled web surrounding Pedro's death.

He adjusted himself in his chair, buttoned his shirt collar, and cleared some space on the desk, which was crowded with papers. Odete walked in through the door, clutching her purse with both hands, her demeanor a mix of anxiety and resolve.
"How can I help you?" the sheriff asked, gesturing for her to sit down.
"I'm not sure, but... I think I may have been the one who saw Pedro for the last time," she said, her voice trembling slightly.

# Thirty-Two

The sheriff listened attentively as Odete recounted being Tadeu's neighbor and occasionally seeing Pedro visit his house. "The last time I saw him, he went in, but I didn't see him leave," she said, her brow furrowing in concern.

This revelation was enough for the sheriff to decide to visit Tadeu's house for an interrogation. He thanked the elderly woman for her proactive approach and handed her his card. "Please call me if you remember anything else," he said, his tone encouraging.

★ ★ ★ ★ ★

Antunes knocked on Tadeu's door, which was unlocked. He remembered Tadeu well, Walmir's son. He'd been a troublesome teenager, and Antunes could recall several incidents involving local kids where Tadeu's name had come up. It was remarkable how he was always somehow involved, always in the company of the wrong crowd. When the other Tadeu opened the door, he tried to appear calm, but inside, he was a bundle of nerves. He couldn't afford any slip-ups in his story.

"How can I help you?" he asked, forcing a smile.

"I need to ask you some questions about Pedro. May I come in?" Antunes replied, eyeing the young man closely.

"*No, you can't come in,*" was the first thought that crossed Tadeu's mind. But instead, he gestured for the sheriff to enter, suppressing his anxiety. "Sure, please have a seat," he offered, leading Antunes to the living room.

As the sheriff settled onto the sofa, he observed the well-kept room. Despite knowing that Tadeu didn't have a significant job, the furniture was nice and the space was tidy, which piqued Antunes's curiosity. How could he afford such quality items?

"Nice place you've got here," Antunes commented casually, trying to gauge Tadeu's reaction.

"Thanks," Tadeu replied, his heart racing. "I try to keep it organized."

Antunes leaned forward, his demeanor shifting to a more serious tone. "I'm here about Pedro. We found him... well, you probably know."

The other Tadeu offered him something to drink, but Antunes politely declined. He rummaged through his coat pocket and pulled out a notepad and a pen.

"Alright, Tadeu," he began, "I have a few questions for you. They're straightforward and won't take long. Did you know Pedro?"

"Yes, I knew him," Tadeu replied.

"Were you childhood friends?"

"Not exactly. He was younger than I am. We had mutual acquaintances, but I wouldn't say we were friends."

"Understood. When was the last time you saw him, and under what circumstances?" The detective began jotting down notes swiftly.

"Well, he came to my house," Tadeu admitted, knowing he couldn't lie about that; he was certain the detective already had that information. "We talked a bit about a project he wanted to start, and then he left."

"What kind of project?" Antunes inquired, pen poised over his notepad.

"Nothing major. He was thinking of starting a business in buying and selling rural land. He needed someone trustworthy to work with him, so I volunteered. I could use the extra income."

"Your house seems quite comfortable for someone in need of extra income."

"Yes, my parents left me good savings when they died." It was a lie. The other Tadeu had occasionally made money transporting drugs for Pedro. It wasn't a frequent gig, but when he accepted the job, he received a substantial sum for each load delivered safely.

"Do you know if Pedro mentioned this plan to anyone else? Who else might be able to confirm your story?"

"He didn't tell anyone; he wanted to structure the business first before discussing it with his parents. He wanted to surprise them, to show that he was becoming independent and capable of being a successful entrepreneur, setting up his own office and everything else."

Tadeu felt he couldn't conjure a more believable story. The region was dotted with farms, and the wealthiest residents were all farmers. Pedro knew these people well, so it made sense for him to pursue that line of work.

The detective remained skeptical. The narrative had some merit, but he couldn't understand why Pedro would seek out someone he wasn't close to as his right-hand man. It also seemed illogical to keep such a venture hidden from his parents, who would surely be able to introduce him to influential clients and support him in his new endeavor.

"Do you know if Pedro had any conflicts with anyone? Have you heard any stories about that?"

"I didn't know him well enough to be aware of such things."

Antunes left a card with Tadeu, asking him to contact him if he recalled anything else. Before getting into his car, he took one last look at Tadeu's house. Something about it told him that the young man wasn't trustworthy. Tadeu, meanwhile, was left panting, his nerves getting the better of him.

# Thirty-Three

Tadeu was consumed by hatred. He felt angry for being a failure, for being the son of a deranged man who saw things that weren't there and vented his madness by beating his devoted and loving wife. He seethed at all the poor choices he had made. He should have left town when he was still young, when he had the energy to start over from scratch. Now it was too late; even though he was still young, he lacked the willpower to change.

On the floor lay the suitcase he had started to pack after witnessing the murder committed by the other Tadeu. Where had his mind been? Where could he possibly go? He laughed at himself, but it was a laugh steeped in despair.

He was alone, with no friends left. He could no longer visit Ivone's house—who knew what Beto had told her? And Cintia had accepted that son of a bitch's apologies. How could he have fallen in love with such a weak-minded woman?

Yet, even amidst his anger, Tadeu's feelings for Cintia remained unchanged. He was simply too furious at that moment to acknowledge them.

He headed to the market, his fridge completely bare—there wasn't even a drop of water left. He planned to buy enough food to last him several days, not wanting to step outside again anytime soon. He needed to find a way to interact with the other Tadeu; he had devised an elaborate plan and was determined to put it into action. After making his purchases, he wrote a note and attached it to Max's collar. Then he set the dog food bag down in front of Ivone's house, saying, "Take care of me. My owner will be away for a few days. And if he doesn't come back, I'll be very happy if you let me live here."

**✻ ✻ ✻ ✻ ✻**

Days slipped by without a single visitor or phone call for Tadeu. This was it—this was the existence of someone deemed entirely dispensable by society. He had quit his job days earlier, and not even his boss had bothered to insist that he stay.

What a disgrace of a man he had become.

* * * * *

Tadeu was dozing on the couch when he heard the door to his room creak open. There he stood: the other Tadeu.

Finally.

They locked eyes, and the other Tadeu let out a heavy sigh, his expression serious. For several days, he had caught glimpses of Tadeu in that living room—depressed, forlorn, sprawled on the couch—even if only for brief moments. He shook his head, his voice firm.

"I don't know what's going on, but this needs to stop. I don't want to live like this anymore. My life is a mess, and..."

"You don't want to live like this anymore? You've got it damn good. It's not you who's been stuck at home for days without a single phone call. Look at your living room: that fancy TV of yours, and those expensive playboy clothes. I know where your money comes from; I know you're just as messed up as I am. The only difference is that you didn't have Beto messing up your life."

The other Tadeu frowned, irritated. He wasn't responsible for this stranger's miserable existence. Everything had already been chaotic enough; who did this guy think he was to show up out of nowhere and start spouting nonsense?

ut then Tadeu realized that in both versions of his life, he hadn't become a decent person. That realization made him a failure in doubles. At least in the other life, he had achieved a better financial situation—and he had Cintia.

* * * * *

The two identical men stood in the living room of the house they both inhabited simultaneously. Neither desired this encounter anymore; both longed to leave and start anew. They suspected that if they never entered that house again, they could move on peacefully with their lives.

The other Tadeu returned from the kitchen, a glass of whiskey nearly filled to the brim, ice absent.

"Tell me more about your life," he said, a hint of curiosity in his tone. "I could be in your shoes right now, you know? If it weren't for Beto, that jerk. Always excelling at everything, always better at everything. Why did he think that reporting me to the police would be good for me? It's easy to get things when you have your parents' support and their money to study abroad..."

The other Tadeu wasn't quite sure to whom he was referring. His friend—the other Beto—would never do that to him. Sure, Beto was a bit odd and methodical, didn't have many friends, and was rather quiet. But he was hardworking, ambitious, and deserving of a great future, not someone inclined to ruin another person's life.

Tadeu sat on the sofa in the living room, but it wasn't his living room; it was the other Tadeu's. The rug was nicer, the paint fresh. The TV was different, though the furniture arrangement was almost the same. Even the scent in the air was better. A picture frame on the wall held a photo of Cintia.

His heart raced, and drops of sweat began to form on his forehead; he could feel his skin warming. He felt suffocated in that setting, inferior. Everywhere he looked, everything was better than in his own home.

The other Tadeu approached, looking at him with pity, as if he were a frightened little puppy. Tadeu struggled to breathe; he couldn't feel the air filling his lungs. Panic set in. What was happening? He felt dizzy, his vision blurred.

He had been confined to that house for days, eating poorly and constantly drunk. To top it off, he had taken some psychotropic pills in a futile attempt to relax and sleep. A small stash still lingered in the back of the closet from when teenagers used to come to him, mixing their medications with alcohol for a different kind of high.

He grabbed a long-necked beer bottle from the coffee table and took a sip. It was warm, the taste was awful, and he grimaced.

"Even this shitty beer tastes bad," he muttered.

He had nothing left to lose; he had already lost everything. In a burst of rage, he sprang from the sofa and, in the most cowardly manner possible, acted on a violent instinct that was foreign to him.

He struck the other Tadeu on the head. The glass shattered against the man's forehead, cutting the skin and causing blood to gush out instantly. The other Tadeu staggered, closing his eyes against the blood flowing down his face, reaching out with one hand in search of support while using the other to wipe his forehead. Then he was struck again from behind. Tadeu had hit him with a chair that had been leaning in the corner of the room. Another blow followed. And another.

Tadeu panted, pouring all his strength into the attack until he could continue no longer. He paused to catch his breath, glancing down to check if the other Tadeu was still breathing.

He was dead. Cowardly murdered, just like Pedro a few days ago. The same type of attack.

His plan was complete. If he couldn't have the life that had been ruthlessly stolen from him by Beto, then no one else would either. If he couldn't have Cintia, he couldn't bear the thought of another Tadeu having her.

He wrapped the corpse in the living room carpet, contemplating how to dispose of it. He left the body in the laundry room while he considered his next move. Maybe he wouldn't need to do anything at all. He could simply return to his life and let someone else—perhaps Cintia, the other one—discover the body. Let them deal with it.

He took a shower, letting the hot water cascade down his back and face, tightly closing his eyes. He hoped that when he opened them again, he would be back home, with no more encounters with the other Tadeu, everything resolved.

# Thirty Four

When Tadeu opened his eyes, the bathroom remained unchanged. Nothing had shifted. He wasn't in his usual house; he was still in the other Tadeu's, the one that was beautifully furnished and well-decorated.

He put on clothes he found in the closet—surprisingly well-fitting and brand new. He liked what he saw in the mirror.

The other Tadeu's body still lay rolled up in the carpet. He didn't have a car to transport it... or did he? He suddenly remembered that the other Tadeu had a car.

It was parked in the garden. He found the key in the corpse's pants pocket. He would have to leave at a time when there were as few people on the street as possible. He spent the night sharing the room with the body, ignoring his phone when it rang. He still wasn't ready to talk.

As twilight enveloped the city, bringing with it the damp mist of dawn, he opened the trunk and placed the body inside.

What a damn heavy corpse.

He drove to the place where he used to camp with Beto: the abandoned power plant trail. There was a spot behind a massive rock formation where no one would find the body as quickly as they had found Pedro's—perhaps never.

He dug for about two hours, finally concluding that the hole was deep enough. But he couldn't just bury the other Tadeu's body like that, risking it being discovered and recognized someday. He had brought a machete with him. With grim determination, he disfigured the man's face until it became a shapeless, unrecognizable mass. He had brought a few tools with him. As he drove to the location, he tried to imagine every possible scenario and how he would ensure the body wouldn't be discovered and if it were, that it wouldn't be easily identified. He took a deep breath and, with pliers in hand, pulled out all of his teeth. It wasn't an easy task; in fact, it was far more difficult than he had imagined. The blood wouldn't stop pulsing, everything was filthy, soaked in the red liquid. At times, he closed his eyes in an attempt not to see the teeth coming out. He felt nauseated; his stomach churned. Dismembering a body requires immense strength, and he was already exhausted, but the adrenaline and the fear of getting caught still gave him enough fuel to keep going.

After gathering all the teeth he had managed to pull out, he shoved them into his pocket, deciding he'd figure out what to do with them later. With the same machete he had used to disfigure the corpse's face, he cut off all his fingers to make it harder to collect fingerprints, tossing the little pieces into the river. He was tired. His muscles ached from the sheer force he had needed to use throughout the process. He stared at the shapeless mass on the floor, what lay there was no longer a body, and certainly not a person. It was nothing more than a pile of blood-soaked remains, stripped of identity, stripped of life. Of all the times Tadeu had felt anger toward someone, he had never imagined he would let that anger consume him to this extent, let alone take him this far. He hadn't just killed a person with his own hands, he had made sure that what was left was utterly unrecognizable.

Exhausted and filthy, he covered the body with dirt.

Afterward, he washed his hands and face in the frigid river. The freezing water didn't wash away all the traces, only enough so that he could get into the car without making too much of a mess. Morning had already broken. The city was waking up in peace.

* * * * *

Back home again, he set about cleaning up the mess. Glass shards, blood, pieces of the broken chair—everything lay scattered around the room.

By the time he finished, with the dead man's cell phone in hand, he responded to dozens of messages from Cintia. He concocted a story about having drunk too much, falling asleep, waking up with a terrible hangover, taking some anti-nausea medication, and going back to sleep, explaining that he had stayed in bed longer than he should have. He fielded countless questions and offered apologies for not keeping in touch.

Women. Exhausted, he lay down on the unfamiliar bed and fell into a deep sleep, like a rock. He was so drained that he passed out before he had a chance to process everything that had happened. That problem would have to wait until he woke up.

# Thirty-Five

Tadeu woke up naturally, the sunlight intruding on his eyes. He was still in the other house. Stretching out on the balcony, he felt a lingering exhaustion.

Ivone waved from across the garden, her cheerful voice carrying over. "Good morning, my angel!" Tadeu returned the gesture, unsure of how to navigate this new reality. He walked along the cobblestone street, making his way to the town square. Everything felt slightly different; the garden had been rearranged, and the fountain glistened with fresh paint.

The bandstand had been beautifully restored.

The bakery owner was the same, as was the bar owner. The man selling cotton candy and the popcorn cart vendor were familiar faces. He settled onto a bench, trying to find a sense of calm, but his mind raced with thoughts: *What have I done?*

How long would he be trapped in this life, in a life that wasn't truly his? As he pondered, he realized he had no desire to return to his old life. Wasn't that what he had yearned for months? Could this be his fresh start? He closed his eyes and inhaled deeply, acknowledging that he would need to adapt.

He had longed for this moment enough to finally grasp it. Ironically, he hadn't been prepared at all.

But he would figure it out.

In his previous life, he had quarreled with Beto, leading to a gradual estrangement from Cintia and Ivone. There was no one left to miss him. Days had slipped by in isolation, his phone silent and void of calls. Not a single one. If someone were to search for him, they would find an empty house, a testament to his departure without a glance back, without so much as an explanation.

Perhaps this way, he would at least become a legend on that street. A quiet smile tugged at his lips as he reassured himself that Max would be fine. In this new reality, there was no other Max to keep him company. He knew the dog would be well cared for by Beto's mother, but he would miss him terribly. Unfortunately, he had made a choice—and what he had decided did not include Max.

* * * * *

*"I could get used to this."*
That was his first thought when he checked his bank account. He wasn't a millionaire, but there was a reasonable amount saved. Enough to last him a few years, as long as he invested it wisely. In a few days, he would see Cintia, and the thought made him feel strangely anxious. He recalled that the other Tadeu had plans to move in with her in the capital. It seemed like the perfect opportunity—to leave, distance himself from all of this, and finally start over. He would continue the other Tadeu's plans.
But doubts crept in. Would Cintia notice anything? Would she sense that something was different? His smell, his touch, his kiss— would they be the same? How much, really, were he and the other Tadeu alike? How much were they truly the same person... or just two men who happened to look alike?
Regardless of the answer, he knew one thing for sure, he and the other version of himself were more alike than he wanted to admit. At the height of his problems, he had cowardly murdered someone, just as the other Tadeu had done. In every version of his life, he knew he was a killer.
But that didn't matter anymore. What mattered now was that he would be with Cintia, that he'd be friends with Beto again. He would buy a German shepherd.

* * * * *

Cintia entered through the living room door as Tadeu finished tidying up the kitchen. He wanted everything to be perfect to impress her. He heard the thud of her suitcase landing on the sofa. His heart raced as he wiped his hands on the dishcloth. He took a deep breath. *This is it.*

They had agreed to spend the weekend together in the countryside. Ivone had invited the four of them for dinner: Beto and Aline, Tadeu and Cintia. It would be Tadeu's first time meeting Aline, who in his other life had been Beto's married lover—the reason the two of them had fought that day at the bakery.

Cintia kissed him on the lips, as girlfriends usually do, but the moment sent a chill down his spine. He was tense, almost trembling, but he couldn't let it show. He could hardly believe he was touching her, feeling the warmth of her smooth skin. Her light brown hair was tied up in a ponytail, casually resting on top of her head. Tadeu hugged her for a long time, holding on as if grounding himself in this new reality.

For now, she hadn't noticed anything wrong.

"I missed you," she said with a provocative look.

"Me too," he replied, keeping his words brief, trying to maintain his composure.

"Then come," Cintia said, pulling him by the hand toward the bedroom. "I want to enjoy this afternoon with you before we go to dinner with Ivone."

Tadeu let himself be led, his mind racing. He felt the tension in his body but forced himself to relax. This was the moment he had been waiting for, the chance to completely step into the other Tadeu's life. He just needed to make sure that nothing gave him away.

# Thirty-Six

The police chief investigating Pedro's death appeared on television, giving an interview. He mentioned that there were some suspects and that soon he could provide more definitive updates on the case. Tadeu felt the weight of that statement—he still needed to deal with this situation. He wasn't guilty of Pedro's murder, but he didn't want to pay for a crime he didn't commit. All he wanted was to get out of trouble as quickly as possible.

At times, he feared he would be caught, imagining a lifetime in jail for something he hadn't done. Well... he had killed the other Tadeu. Being caught for Pedro's death would almost feel like a form of cosmic justice, a kind of universal compensation. But even that wouldn't be fair. Killing the other Tadeu hadn't impacted anyone else's life but his own. No one in his old life missed him. In fact, in the reality he had left behind, Pedro was still alive.

The thought gave him an odd sense of detachment. In a way, he'd escaped from a life that no longer existed, and now he was living someone else's.

He remembered that when he had witnessed the murder committed by the other Tadeu, Pedro's revolver had been stored in a secret compartment in a piece of furniture in the living room. Desperation surged through him as he rummaged through the drawers, his hands shaking until he found the gun. Cold and heavy, it felt like the final piece of a puzzle he no longer wanted to solve. He would do this in the most cowardly way possible. He had nothing left to lose.

Without thinking twice, he grabbed the revolver, slipped it into his jacket pocket, and headed for the door. His mind raced as he got in the car, the weight of the weapon feeling like a ticking bomb. He drove towards the former mayor's house, where everything had begun. His heart pounded in his chest, and his thoughts were a chaotic blur, but one thing was certain: there was no turning back now. Lately, with everything that had been happening, Tadeu had become far more impulsive. A constant sense of urgency gnawed at him. He felt the need to solve everything as quickly as possible, just to be free from his problems as soon as possible. The urge to finally start living his new life and leave the old one behind overwhelmed him, crashing into him like a wave. It felt as though, at any moment, everything could go back to the way it was, unless he thought fast and acted even faster.

★ ★ ★ ★ ★

He rang the doorbell. Within seconds, the maid appeared at the gate, looking around cautiously, searching for whoever the visitor might be.

"I need to speak with the owner of the house, please."

"Who is this?" she asked, eyeing him with curiosity.

"Please tell him it's Tadeu, Cintia's boyfriend—he knows who that is. He'll want to hear about this; it's something that means a lot to him."

After a brief moment, the maid returned with keys in hand, opened the gate, and gestured for Tadeu to follow her. She led him to the living room, a vast space adorned with expensive yet questionably tasteful decorations. The room was filled with stylish armchairs and featured a genuine leather sofa, but nothing seemed to match. On a corner table sat a tray with glasses, ice, and various drinks. The carpet was burgundy, chandeliers hung from the ceiling, and the windows were large, covered with heavy fabric curtains. It was obvious that everything there was supposedly expensive, but not necessarily tasteful. Maybe it had been, at some point back in the 1970s.

"What can I do for you?" the former mayor asked as he entered the room, his brows furrowed while finishing buttoning up his coat, clearly thrown on in a hurry, as he certainly hadn't been expecting visitors at that moment.

"Talk," Tadeu replied, taking a deep breath. "Talk about Pedro."

The ex-mayor's eyes widened.

"What do you mean?" he asked, his voice tinged with disbelief. Just take me somewhere in this house where no one can overhear us, please."

The man wasn't yet sure what this was all about, but he could tell by the tone of the young man's voice that something serious was coming, and he respected that. Still wary, the man led Tadeu to his office, a dimly lit room lined with wooden shelves packed with books. A mahogany desk sat at the center, positioned atop a cowhide rug. "The police suspect I have something to do with your son's death," Tadeu began, his voice steady. "Pedro was at my house on the day he disappeared, but the truth is we were planning to start a business together. He wanted to work in rural land sales but didn't want to tell you yet." He delivered the lie smoothly, having rehearsed extensively in front of the mirror.

"How so? He never mentioned anything to me about that." The father's surprise was evident in his furrowed brow.

"Well, it turns out that your son was involved in drug trafficking. I know people who can confirm this. He was probably mixed up in some trouble, owing money to someone. Whoever killed him must be dangerous." Tadeu knew the names of some drug dealers, although his direct contact had been with Pedro himself.

The father listened, incredulous but not entirely surprised by the news. Over the years, he had discovered marijuana, cocaine, and ecstasy among his son's belongings. However, he had never let the news leak, determined to protect their family name. They were too traditional a family to get involved in such scandals.

The ex-mayor avoided meeting Tadeu's eyes.

"I don't know what to say. We have to inform the police..."

"No, we're not going to inform the police. I don't want to get involved in the investigations. I'm not crazy enough to mess with these people. I have messages on my phone from your son, asking me to help him sell drugs. He's been in this for some time."

"Wait, asking you? But... what about the land business?"

Tadeu realized he had let a critical detail slip and couldn't backtrack now. He stuck to his lie.

"Well... after I did some jobs for him, he started trusting me to work on more serious things together. To tell the truth, I suspect he needed a way to launder money."

"Launder money? What money? If it was money he needed, he could have just talked to me. I have money, lots of it..."

The man seemed incredulous. As much as he doubted the story, he also wouldn't be surprised if it turned out to be true. "Yes, and that's what we're going to talk about now." Tadeu reached for the gun at his waist, not aiming it at Pedro's father but holding it parallel to his body. The ex-mayor startled and instinctively took a step back.

"I don't understand. What do you want?" the man said, slowly raising his hands to show he was trying to cooperate, no matter how absurd the situation seemed.

"What I want is very simple. You said you have a lot of money, so you're going to use that money to get my name out of this investigation."

"What do you mean?"

"Well... I know it, you know it, everybody knows that Detective Antunes isn't exactly the most honest guy. Everyone knows he can be bought off easily. I know he's arrested and released people in this town for peanuts." Tadeu was referring to his own experience, remembering how Beto had turned him in, deliberately leaving him imprisoned for a few days.

"I'm not going to do that! My son was brutally murdered, and I will find out who did it, no matter what it takes. Who do you think you are to ask me something like this?"

Tadeu had anticipated that he would face resistance. He had crafted his performance, knowing that he only had one chance to make it work. He couldn't afford to fail. He couldn't. Not at all. He raised the gun to chest height, watching the gleam it reflected from the chandelier. He stared at that reflection for long seconds before looking into the face of the man standing defenseless before him.

"We'll do the following: you're going to talk to the detective. I don't know what you'll propose to him, and I don't care. He's going to clear my name from this investigation; he won't come looking for me anymore. Otherwise, I'll be forced to make two decisions I won't like. First, I'll show all the messages Pedro sent me, arranging drug deliveries to other cities. The newspapers will go crazy when they find out about this. I bet they'll publish all our conversations in full. Your political enemies will destroy you and your family. How will you explain to the press that your son was feeding all the drug trafficking in this region and was responsible for the addiction of hundreds of minors?"

He took a deep breath and continued, "See this gun? I won't hesitate to use it, whether on you, your wife, or your remaining little daughter."

"I can't believe Cintia is dating a guy like you," the man said, shaking his head in dismay, his gaze lost within the office.

"And I can't believe your precious son was involved with drug dealers. You know, if this story leaks, your reputation is finished, right? You'll never be able to run for anything again. Who knows how much this filthy press here will charge to not publish the contents of my phone? Do you want Pedro to be remembered for generations as the incompetent junkie who was brutally and cowardly murdered over a supposed drug debt? I think that could stain your family name for a long time. I can already hear this story being exploited endlessly on every true crime podcast out there."

* * * * *

Tadeu finally managed to breathe once he left the former mayor's house. He considered getting rid of the gun but ultimately chose to keep it, uncertain of how things would unfold. He stood still in front of the enormous gate, his gaze unfocused, his hands trembling. He had needed to adopt a demeanor that felt entirely unnatural to him. "*I'm not like this, but I had to do it. It was necessary,*" he thought.

# Thirty-Seven

Christmas was approaching, and Tadeu was driving to the capital without Cintia's knowledge, planning a surprise. He carried a small suede box containing a ring tucked safely in his pocket. His plan was to spend a few days with her in the city, enjoying their time together, and then, when he felt more confident, take her out to dinner at a fancy restaurant and propose. The thought filled him with excitement and a tinge of nervousness; this was a moment he had dreamed about for a long time.

*****

Cintia opened the apartment door and smiled somewhat awkwardly.

"Hi! What a surprise!" Tadeu stepped inside, though he didn't know the place well. He needed to act naturally during the visit; after all, the other Tadeu had been there a few times. They greeted each other with a kiss.

"But what are you doing here?" she asked.

"Oh, I wanted to surprise you. I missed you."

She tried to disguise her discomfort, but Tadeu sensed it. A wave of worry washed over him, leaving him unsure of what he had done wrong. Maybe she was just dealing with a work problem, who knows?

"I came to take you out to dinner. Shall we?" he offered, hoping to lighten the mood.

"Sure, let me just change first," she replied, her tone still a bit hesitant.

*****

The place had been carefully chosen by Tadeu in advance. It was a small Italian restaurant, reminiscent of a cozy bistro, super romantic and perfect for couples. They settled at a wooden table adorned with a red-and-green-checkered tablecloth and ordered two pasta dishes, along with a bottle of wine to share.

"Cintia, I came here to talk to you," he began, trying to steady his nerves. "To see you, of course, but also to discuss something important."

"Yes?" she replied, her eyebrows raised in curiosity.

Tadeu scratched his neck, searching for the right words. "So... I've been thinking. I stay out in the countryside alone, and you're here in the capital. What do you think about me moving here? To be closer to you, you know?" He squeezed his sweaty hands under the table, feeling the anxiety bubble up.

In recent months, Tadeu had felt more fulfilled than ever. He had quickly adapted to his new life and routine. His friendship with Beto had been reignited, and he would be completely happy if he still had the opportunity to live with his stepmother. But unfortunately, not everything could be perfect. Still, he couldn't complain; life was already good enough wonderful, to tell the truth.

"Look, Tadeu," Cintia said, her voice apprehensive as she spun her fork in her empty plate, avoiding his gaze. "I understand that you feel lonely there and all. I don't know how you've managed to stay in that town for so long. But... I hope you want to come here for yourself, and not because of me, you know?" She bit her lip, visibly tense.

Tadeu was taken aback by her response. He had expected her to be happy about the announcement, but instead, it felt like a bucket of cold water had been poured over him. "What... what do you mean?"

"I'm not saying you shouldn't come," she clarified, raising her hands slightly. "I just don't want you to put that responsibility on me. The capital is full of opportunities, and I hope that's the real reason you're considering this."

"Yes, it is! But... I thought you would like what I said! Why are you treating me like this?" he frowned, feeling a knot tighten in his stomach.

"Because when we first got together, I said I didn't want anything serious with anyone. There was a vibe; it was really nice, and I liked you. But then we started getting more involved, and before I knew it, we were practically dating. I don't know if I want to take a bigger step than this. At least not now." She tried to soften the blow, clearly not wanting to hurt him.

"What do you mean by that?" he asked, incredulous. "Spending weekends with me in the countryside... was it some kind of pastime for you?"

"Pastime? No! I like you. I enjoy your company. It's just that... I think we wouldn't work out if we delved deeper into things, you know?"

"No, I don't understand!" His voice raised unintentionally, the frustration bubbling over. Cintia raised her right hand, a silent plea for him to calm down.

"Tadeu, please, I need you to stay calm. And don't act like you don't understand; that's always been our agreement."

The word "agreement" hung in the air, heavy with meaning. Tadeu felt lost, unable to grasp what she was referring to. He hadn't been part of their life the whole time; all he knew was what he had managed to absorb during the fleeting moments he had observed their relationship, her with the other Tadeu.

He could hardly believe he was letting Cintia slip through his fingers like sand. He felt exposed, as if he had taken a fall and became the target of everyone's ridicule, hearing the laughter and seeing fingers pointed at him. He felt ridiculous and embarrassed, like garbage.

Cintia called the waiter, gesturing for the bill. She was visibly irritated, and he didn't know this version of her. He missed her sweetness, her charming smile. This Cintia was tough, too resolved for him.

The couple left the restaurant in silence, the weight of unspoken words hanging heavily between them. Tadeu still hadn't fully grasped the whole situation. His mind was a whirlwind of confusion, and nothing made sense. Maybe he had acted too hastily, perhaps his anxiety and impulsiveness had blinded him to the reality that was actually unfolding.

Now, he felt like an idiot. An idiot who kept making bad decisions one after another. He had become so obsessed with winning Cintia over, to prove that he could "succeed" at least once, that he hadn't even paid attention to what *she actually wanted.*

<h2 style="text-align:center">Thirty-Eight</h2>

As Tadeu had already convinced himself about leaving the countryside, he now intended to follow through with the idea, with or without Cintia. At home, he began packing things into boxes. *I'll take some time away; she'll calm down, realize she doesn't want to be without me, and everything will work out,* he thought, trying to maintain a positive outlook at all costs. He didn't want to give up, didn't want to succumb to the idea that all was lost. No!

Ivone appeared at the window, her expression somber. She would miss one of her dearest neighbors. Everyone was leaving, and with each passing day, her sense of loneliness deepened.

"I'll miss you, Tadeu," she said, her voice choked with emotion as she held back tears.

"I'll miss you, too... Ivone, you've been and always will be like a mother to me. I know my birth mother abandoned me, and I had the best stepmother anyone could have, but I'll never forget everything you've done for me. I promise I'll come back to visit you often."

Tadeu's words hung in the air, filled with sincerity. He knew he was leaving a piece of his heart behind.

Ivone didn't want to delve further into the conversation, but she found it odd that Tadeu mentioned his mother had abandoned him. She knew the story wasn't quite that simple.

One night, when Tadeu was still a baby, Walmir had returned home so drunk from the bar that he ended up beating Arlete to death. She was rushed to a hospital in a nearby town, where she lingered in a coma for several days, but ultimately, she didn't survive.

Walmir and Márcia were lovers, and it didn't take long for them to openly assume their relationship. Even during the time Walmir spent in jail, convicted of manslaughter, he and Márcia continued their affair. Shortly thereafter, he was granted parole and eventually released. He resumed his life alongside Márcia, leaving behind a trail of pain that echoed through Tadeu's early years.

Ivone shook her head, the weight of the past heavy on her heart. She wanted to comfort Tadeu, to help him see that he was loved and cared for. But some truths were hard to voice, and the memories of that night lingered like shadows in her mind.

It didn't take long for the abuse against her to begin as well.

Ivone sometimes felt guilty for not having spoken the truth when she had the chance. There were moments when she came so close to saying it, but she held back. She didn't want to open that wound. She had the "son" she had always dreamed of, loving and attached to her. She didn't want to push him away, to lose him. She preferred to keep silent. That was the price she was willing to pay. If one day everything came to light, she would find a way to deal with it; otherwise, she would move on with her life, sharing only what was convenient for her.

Ivone spent the rest of the afternoon keeping Tadeu company. The affection between them was palpable, a bond forged through years of shared experiences and mutual care. Tadeu could never understand Beto's indifference in the face of the great fortune of having a mother like Ivone.

"Tomorrow, I expect you at my house with a homemade goodbye pie. I'll wrap it up nicely for you to take to the city," she said with a warm smile.

Tadeu's eyes lit up at the thought. He didn't know what he would do without Ivone by his side, caring for him like she always had. He would miss her dearly. If he could, he would take her with him. But the reality was stark: he would need to give up some things to advance in others. He understood that life was about sacrifices, but the thought of leaving Ivone behind felt like tearing a piece of his heart out.

As he packed, he tried to hold onto the memories they had created together, hoping that they would sustain him in the new life he was stepping into.

★ ★ ★ ★ ★

Tadeu and Cintia weren't speaking. He waited for her to call or message, but that didn't happen, which made him extremely nervous.

He blamed himself for rushing things between them. Had he scared Cintia off? He couldn't lose her, especially now when he felt so close to finally winning her over for good. So close.

He had never been good with women. In moments like these, he wished he had Beto's confidence and charm. Beto would surely know what to do. With a sigh, Tadeu dialed his friend's number, feeling a sense of urgency.

"Hey, can we meet up?" Tadeu asked when Beto answered.

"Of course. What's going on?" Beto replied, his tone shifting to concern.

"I just need to talk. Can we grab a drink?"

"Absolutely. I'll pick you up in thirty."

As Tadeu hung up, a knot of anxiety tightened in his stomach. He needed guidance, and he hoped that Beto could help him navigate the mess he'd made of things with Cintia.

★ ★ ★ ★ ★

Tadeu was amazed by Beto's apartment. He hadn't imagined his friend had such good taste. As he looked around, he spotted an extremely soft shaggy rug that made him think that he could sleep there every day. Abstract paintings of various sizes adorned the walls, and the sleek black leather sofa had a modern design. In one corner stood a chic coffee maker on an exclusive piece of furniture, and, of course, there was a bar filled with impressive and expensive drinks.

Beto poured two glasses of whiskey and handed one to Tadeu. He took a sip and let out a sigh of relief; he was exhausted from a long day at the office. Beto had been dating Aline for some time, which complicated his ability to offer solid advice about Cintia. Still, he was willing to help based on his own experiences.

"I'm no expert on the subject, Tadeu, but from what you've told me..." he began, hesitating slightly. "It's tough to say this, but... it seems like there's no turning back."

"No turning back? How can there be no turning back? There has to be a way!" Tadeu protested, his voice rising with desperation.

"Women are crazy about dating, getting married, having kids. This Cintia... I don't know. Was she really in love with you?" Beto asked, tilting his head slightly as he regarded Tadeu.

"I believed she was," Tadeu replied, a hint of uncertainty creeping into his voice.

"You've been together for a few months, right?" Beto continued, swirling the whiskey in his glass. "I had little contact with her; we went out a few times for dinner with other friends. It's hard to say this, but since you asked for my opinion, I feel obligated to mention... I've never seen Cintia making plans for the two of you, you know? She used to visit you every weekend... But did you ever talk about building a life together, for instance?"

"No... never," Tadeu admitted, his heart sinking. In truth, he didn't have any evidence to suggest that Cintia shared those aspirations. He thought back over the time they had spent together, but nothing suggested that they were heading in that direction.

Beto stirred his whiskey-filled glass, savoring each sip while he thought. "Well, it's tricky to encourage you to go after her. Look at Aline, for example... When we met, she was married. She left her husband to be with me, and now she keeps dropping hints that she wants to get married again."

Tadeu felt a pang of annoyance, the truth cutting deeper than he expected. How could it be that Cintia didn't love him? For almost a year, she had traveled to the countryside every weekend; they had shared so much together, gone out, and had the best sex he had ever experienced. The idea that she could remain indifferent after all that felt like a punch to the gut. He couldn't comprehend how, after so much time, she still wasn't in love with him.

He couldn't accept the reality that, in every version of his life, Cintia didn't reciprocate his love. The thought gnawed at him, a relentless ache in his chest.

"Thanks, man, but... I'm not feeling too well. I'm going back to the hotel. Thanks," he said, cutting their conversation short.

His feelings towards her were a tangled mess. As much as Tadeu loved her madly, he was overwhelmed by sadness and anger. He pictured how things could go if they were together again, how he might yell at her, humiliate her for not feeling the same way, but he knew that once the anger faded, he would want nothing more than to hug her, cry, and apologize for the outburst.

At least this time she wasn't with Beto. That thought offered a flicker of comfort. He stepped out of the apartment and into the cool night air, his mind swirling with memories of laughter, shared moments, and the warmth of her presence. Each memory felt like a weight dragging him down, making it hard to breathe.

# Thirty-Nine

Tadeu had already received several calls from people interested in buying the house he had listed. He had priced it below market value, eager to offload the burden quickly. Leaving a copy of the keys with Ivone, he ensured that she could let potential buyers in for viewings. Once a month, he would make the trip to the countryside to mow the lawn and tidy up the place, always stopping by Beto's mother's house for a chat.

His relationship with Cintia remained rocky. They were slowly starting to communicate again, but she still seemed defensive, and Tadeu felt uncertain about how to navigate the situation. So he decided to let her take the lead, allowing fate to shape his future.

On a particularly gray Saturday, he found himself raking dry leaves from the lawn of his old house. The "for sale" sign creaked and swayed in the chilly wind, while the sky hung heavy and whitish, threatening rain at any moment.

Odete, as always, watched him from her window, her silhouette framed against the dim light inside. In this new phase of his life, Tadeu wasn't sure if he had forged any real friendship with her; if anything, it seemed more like a silent understanding borne from their shared history in the neighborhood. Despite her watchful presence, he felt the distance between them, a barrier built from years of isolation and unspoken words.

He gave a small wave to the old woman, accompanied by a sheepish smile, but she didn't respond. Instead, she abruptly closed the brown fabric curtain, only to appear moments later on the lawn.

"You don't fool me now, you never did," she declared, pointing a gnarled finger at him. "That young man, the son of the former mayor, I always saw him around here..."

"Look, Odete, I don't know what you're trying to suggest, but I have nothing to do with him or his death, if that's what you're insinuating..." He wasn't sure, but he had the feeling that Odete had just threatened him.

"Indolent, just like his father. Lucky for you, I can't prove anything. And even if I could, this useless police force we have around here wouldn't lift a finger to solve the case. We're all damned," she grumbled, her usual grumpiness on full display.

Tadeu felt a pang of discomfort at her words. He had managed to escape guilt for the crime the other Tadeu had committed, thanks to an incompetent, lazy, and corrupt detective, as well as a disgusting, vain, and selfish family, a family that preferred to ignore their son's murder rather than confront their own shortcomings.

It wouldn't be fair for him to pay the price for that. Yet he had to consider the very real possibility of Odete causing bigger problems. He couldn't let his plans unravel because of her incessant meddling. Tightening his grip on the rake, he steeled himself against the tension that hung in the air, aware that he had to find a way to sidestep her scrutiny while maintaining his carefully constructed facade.

Tadeu watched as Odete walked through the garden toward his house. The street was empty, and the silence amplified his racing heart. Without thinking, he rushed after her and forced his way into the hallway just before she could close the door. Odete jumped, eyes wide with shock.

"What do you want?" she stammered.

"Listen here, Odete," Tadeu began, his voice low but intense. "I don't know what your problem is with me. I had absolutely nothing to do with that boy's death. I couldn't care less about him."

Odete shrank back as Tadeu leaned closer, feeling an unexpected rush of aggression.

"You're just a lonely, gossiping old woman," he continued, his voice rising. "You do nothing useful for this town. You've never done anything useful for anyone on this street. I'm leaving this shitty place, and you're not going to stop me. You're not going to stop me!"

He shouted the last words, feeling a mixture of anger and disbelief at his own outburst. Just months ago, in his other life, he had helped her with a hurt knee after she fell in front of the bakery. That Tadeu would have never spoken to her like this. The sharp contrast between his past kindness and present rage struck him like a slap.

Odete's expression changed from shock to fear, her lips trembling. Tadeu could see the uncertainty in her eyes, and for a moment, the weight of his actions hit him. But the desperation to escape the life he had inherited, the fear of being ensnared by Odete's suspicions, overshadowed any guilt he felt.

"Stay out of my business, Odete," he warned, taking a step back to regain control of the situation. "If you know what's good for you, you'll keep your mouth shut. I have no qualms about ensuring that you do."

With that, he turned and stormed out. As he stepped into the cool air outside, adrenaline coursed through him, mingling with the regret that was beginning to gnaw at the edges of his mind.

Odete stood her ground, her fear transforming into a defiant resolve. "Do whatever you want, my dear," she said coolly. "You'll have to live with your conscience."

The loud thud of the door echoed in the silence of the street, leaving Tadeu standing outside, feeling a mix of anger and confusion.

He was becoming someone else, and the realization sent a chill down his spine. Was it the toxic environment around him that was poisoning his mind? Or was he tapping into a hidden side of his personality that had lain dormant? Either way, he felt a dark change brewing within him.

As he stood there, he was haunted by the gravity of his actions. Just months ago, he had been a man of principles, someone who helped others. Now he was capable of killing to seize a life that didn't belong to him, and here he was, threatening an elderly woman in her own home.

He closed his eyes, feeling the weight of his choices pressing down on him. *I'm not like this. I'm not like this.* The mantra ran through his mind like a lifeline, a desperate plea to remember who he had once been.

But as the chill of the evening air seeped into his bones, he felt the tug of darkness pulling him deeper. The choices he had made, the life he had assumed, were beginning to shape him in ways he had never anticipated. Taking a deep breath, he tried to center himself. *I need to find my way back,* he thought. *I can't let this place change me completely.*

With that, he turned away from the house, the confrontation leaving a bitter taste in his mouth, vowing to hold on to the remnants of the person he once was, even as he stood at the edge of a precipice.

# Forty

Tadeu spent Christmas alone. With no news from Cintia, he felt no inclination to celebrate anything special. He polished off the entire bottle of whiskey he had on the shelf, seeking solace in its warmth. The new apartment remained unfurnished, cardboard boxes strewn everywhere, a testament to his disarray. Beto was preoccupied with his girlfriend's family, and Ivone had gone to dinner with Beatriz—Cintia's mother—and, consequently, with Cintia herself.

No matter how hard he tried, he felt out of place. Regret for his impulsive move lingered in his thoughts. He had managed to ruin his relationship with Cintia and found himself envious of Beto, who was happily dating a lovely girl.

Now he pondered whether everyone's destiny was predetermined, if everything was already written and could not be altered according to individual desires. What will happen will happen, and that was that.

Self-esteem had never been his strong suit, and now more than ever, he was convinced that he was destined to live in Beto's shadow. This obsession gnawed at him. He hated his friend for betraying him in one life, for being successful in both. He harbored resentment for reasons that couldn't even be rationalized.

How long had he been unhappy? He was perpetually angry, frustrated, and sad. The only moments of joy were with Cintia, the only woman who had ever wanted his company, and even now, she didn't want him anymore. In his old life, he had Max. How he missed Max. It tore at his heart not to be able to see him anymore. He knew Max would be with Ivone, well cared-for. Max had always been his only true friend.

Suddenly, the phone rang, an unknown number flashing on the screen.

"Hello?"

"I'm calling to inquire about the house that's for sale."

"Ah, yes. If you'd like to visit, you can ask the neighbor for the key."

"The neighbor is traveling. She spent New Year's away or something like that. The other neighbor told me he doesn't know when she'll be back."

"I see. Where are you? I'm in the capital. It'll take me at least two hours to get to the house."

"No problem. I'm staying at a relative's house here. When you arrive, please call me back at this same number."

* * * * *

Tadeu drove down the winding road, the rain pouring relentlessly. He parked in front of his old house, a wave of nostalgia washing over him. The closed-up state of Ivone's home gave him an unsettling feeling. He reminded himself not to worry; she was traveling, likely visiting relatives in another city. She was safe and happy.

His gaze swept the street for Odete, but she was absent from her usual post by the window, the brown curtain drawn tight. The street felt eerily deserted, with the other houses seemingly empty as well, likely due to the New Year festivities. Everyone was off somewhere, celebrating. It was early January, yet Tadeu found no excitement for the year ahead.

He lingered by his car, waiting for the caller to arrive. It wasn't long before another vehicle pulled up beside his. A well-dressed man in a suit stepped out and approached him.

"Are you Tadeu? I'm here to see the house."

"Yes, come on in," Tadeu replied, leading the way.

The man introduced himself as Arnaldo, appearing to be in his early fifties. He was in his third marriage and had a young son from this relationship. His wife's family lived in the countryside, and with retirement on the horizon, they planned to move there. Arnaldo was drawn to the house for its large garden and yard, envisioning a peaceful environment for his son, far removed from the dangers of city life. They had even discussed getting a dog.

"The house is in excellent condition and is well-maintained," Tadeu said, gesturing toward the entrance. "The two bedrooms are spacious, and there's ample room in the garden if you want to expand the property or even build a guest house on the same plot." Arnaldo nodded thoughtfully. "I want to surprise my wife. The house isn't huge, but the garden is fantastic, and the street is very quiet. I think she'll like it, but I still need to evaluate the conditions."

"Of course, please feel free," Tadeu replied. "It's a nice place to live, and the neighbors are all good people." He refrained from mentioning Odete, whose presence he had grown to view as more of a burden than a benefit.

Arnaldo seemed convinced, his expression brightening at the prospect. Tadeu felt a surge of hope; he needed this sale to go through. Another opportunity like this might not come along anytime soon in his life, and he was determined to seize it.

# Forty-One

Tadeu said goodbye to Arnaldo, hoping to hear back in a few days. Once inside the house, he began locking the windows and doors that had been opened during the visit. The dark hardwood floor felt cold beneath his feet, and scattered cardboard boxes from the move stood as reminders of his unsettled life. His voice echoed in the empty room, a stark contrast to the silence surrounding him. Empty houses always seemed sad.

Once the sale was finalized, he would finally be free from anything that tethered him to that town. It would be a fresh start. He even entertained the idea of traveling for a while, escaping everything that reminded him of Beto, Cintia, Pedro, and Odete. He needed to come to terms with himself and reflect on all the mistakes he had made. It was difficult to admit that he was struggling in this new life. The cultural baggage he carried from his past was proving insufficient for his current reality.

It had been different for the other Tadeu. That version of himself knew how to navigate life, how to connect with people, and had won Cintia's heart. The other Tadeu had grown up with a different perspective, equipped with the tools to succeed.

He sank to the floor, leaning against one of the bare walls. A shaft of light streamed through the window, illuminating dust particles dancing in the air. Shadows loomed, amplifying his sense of loneliness. Had some people been born solely to fill space, mere extras in the grand play of life? He wondered if he was one of those people. It felt as though he couldn't do anything right, hadn't built anything of significance. Beto thrived in a large company, shaping the futures of many. Cintia was a dentist, dedicated to caring for people's health. And what about him? Did he matter to anyone in his former life, the life that had simply evaporated like smoke? He had no way of knowing the answer, and the uncertainty gnawed at him.

He opened his eyes and felt a sudden chill, an impression of movement lingering in the periphery of his vision. Tadeu blinked, waiting for his eyes to adjust to the dim light filtering through the window. Perhaps it was merely an optical illusion created by the shadows of the trees outside.

But no, it wasn't just a trick of the light. The figure emerged from the kitchen, gradually taking on a more defined shape. As it drew closer, Tadeu could make out the arms, the legs, the clothing, and finally, the face. A wave of terror washed over him; he could hardly believe what he was seeing.

Standing before him was a man: the other Tadeu.

# Forty-Two

For a moment, they simply stared at one another, as if caught in a surreal tableau. The other Tadeu's expression mirrored confusion, perhaps even a hint of curiosity. Tadeu's heart raced. Was he dreaming? Had he lost his mind in the solitude of this empty house?

"How is this possible?" Tadeu stammered, struggling to grasp the reality before him. The other Tadeu remained silent, his gaze unwavering, as if weighing the significance of this unexpected meeting.

He stood up quickly, his heart racing as he glanced around, desperate for something—anything—to use as a shield. He was completely at the mercy of this person who looked just like him.

"So this is what you've become..." the other Tadeu began, his voice dripping with disappointment and disdain.

"Who are you? What do you want with me?" Tadeu shot back, his voice wavering between fear and defiance.

"I thought I'd never see you again after you left," the other Tadeu replied, an unsettling mixture of empathy and contempt in his eyes.

"Leave me alone!" Tadeu yelled, covering his ears, refusing to relive the haunting memories that threatened to overwhelm him.

"There's no way to destroy someone as destroyed as you are," the other Tadeu said, shaking his head in disgust. "Tell me, how did you manage to waste the other chance you had? It's so typical of you. It's so typical of both of us."

"You came back to haunt me, is that it?" Tadeu snapped, his frustration boiling over.

"I didn't come back from anywhere. I'm not the Tadeu you cowardly killed here in this room." He pointed to the spot where the sofa used to be, a gesture that sent a shiver down Tadeu's spine. "I'm the Tadeu who was here, watching everything that happened."

Tadeu's head throbbed, as if a vice were tightening around his temples. He pressed his fingers against the painful area, trying to steady himself. Taking a deep breath, he summoned the courage to ask, "What's going on, after all?"
"A few years ago, I started seeing a man identical to me in my house. This house here," the other Tadeu explained, his voice steady but laced with a hint of desperation. "At first, I was scared. I sought therapy, but over the months, I realized it wasn't helping at all. The therapist didn't believe me, and I didn't feel safe enough to seek another. The visions became more frequent, more vivid and realistic. I realized that they only happened here."

He gestured around the empty room, his hands moving as if to illustrate his point. "I started sharing the house with this other man, watched his life, followed his routine. Suddenly, you appeared, and I thought I had gone completely mad. I started seeing two Tadeus talking to each other," he said, mimicking a puppet show with his hands. "That's when I realized your lives were merging into each other."

Tadeu's heart raced as he processed this revelation.
"I saw when you killed the other Tadeu," the man continued, his eyes narrowing. "I saw when you started living his life as if it were your own. I saw when you got with Cintia, as if you were him. And I also witnessed the moment you returned, devastated from a weekend with her, because you had been rejected."

A silence fell between them, heavy with the weight of the truth. Tadeu felt a chill creep down his spine as the enormity of the situation sank in. "But why?" he asked, his voice barely above a whisper. "Why are you here now?"

The other Tadeu took a step closer, his expression shifting from disappointment to something resembling pity. "I'm here to make you confront what you've done. You can't keep running from your past, Tadeu. You need to face it before you can move on. Otherwise, this cycle will just repeat itself, and neither of us will ever be free."

"Thanks for the audience," Tadeu joked, attempting to diffuse the tension. "Hope you enjoyed the show."

The other Tadeu didn't respond, his gaze fixed on Tadeu with an intensity that made the air between them crackle. With deliberate slowness, he reached for his waist and drew a revolver, aiming it directly at Tadeu.

Tadeu's heart raced, and he instinctively raised his hands, feeling trapped and exposed. A chill crawled down his spine, and his palms began to tingle.

"What are you doing?" he stammered, his voice barely above a whisper.

"Sorry, buddy," the other Tadeu replied, his tone cold. "But of all the lives you've lived, of all the lives I've lived, among all the possibilities of a Tadeu, as sad and lamentable as it may be, your life is still the least worst of all the others."

"Other lives? What others?" Tadeu asked, confusion washing over him.

"Well, there are dozens of Tadeus out there," the other Tadeu explained, his eyes narrowing. "From what I've seen so far, there are many more than I imagined. In fact, they're countless."

"There are others? More others?" Tadeu echoed, his mind racing.

"Yes. Tadeus, Cintias, Betos, and Ivones... I don't know how many; I lost count. All with their mediocre lives, just like me and just like you, living in sync. There are few differences between us, but in essence, we're all the same." He paused, allowing his words to sink in before continuing. "Take Beto, for example. In all possible scenarios, he's an arrogant jerk. Cintia likes to live by appearances, wanting to show that everything's fine, but it never is. She freaks out over any little thing and never manages to find a man who respects her. And you... well, I don't need to say much. You know how we both are two failures. Apparently, failures in every life we live."

Tadeu felt a knot tighten in his stomach. The weight of the other Tadeu's words pressed down on him like a heavy shroud. "But we can change," he pleaded, his voice trembling. "We can break free from this cycle. It doesn't have to be like this."

The other Tadeu's expression remained unreadable, the revolver unwavering in his grip. "Change? Do you really think that's possible? We're trapped in a loop, Tadeu. Every time we try to escape, we just end up back where we started, carrying the same burdens, the same failures. It's time for one of us to end this."

"Is that it? Is this how it ends?" Tadeu asked, his voice filled with despair as he lowered his hands and gazed at the floor. The gravity of the situation crashed down on him. He couldn't fathom being killed by this other Tadeu, a stranger who had just revealed the existence of countless lives, countless versions of himself.

"Looks like it," the other Tadeu replied coolly. "No matter how hard we try to do things differently, it always ends the way it has to end."

Involuntarily, Tadeu took a step forward, driven by a surge of adrenaline. He pushed the other Tadeu against the wall, catching him off-guard. The revolver slipped from the intruder's grasp, clattering to the floor and spinning away from them.

What followed was a chaotic, desperate struggle. Tadeu felt a primal urge to fight for his life, for the fresh start he had yearned for. He refused to hand over that chance to the doppelgänger who seemed intent on snuffing it out.

As they grappled, punches flew in the dim light of the empty living room. Each strike felt like hitting a wall, the other Tadeu's build mirroring his own. It was as if he were fighting a reflection, making it impossible to gain the upper hand.

Tadeu's anger fueled him. He aimed a punch at the other Tadeu's face, but it was met with a block, and their bodies tumbled toward the fallen revolver. In the darkness, it was impossible to tell who was winning. The room felt surreal, shadows dancing around them as they rolled and strained against each other.

Frustration bubbled inside Tadeu. "You don't have to do this!" he shouted between breaths, desperation lacing his voice. "We can find a way out of this mess together!"

But the other Tadeu merely grunted, their bodies entwined in a struggle for survival, each determined to prevail. It was more than just a fight; it was a battle for identity, for the right to define their own path. The weight of their shared existence hung heavy in the air, but Tadeu refused to give up. With one final push, he fought with everything he had, determined to reclaim the life he had fought so hard to build.

The sound of a gunshot shattered the stillness of the empty street, reverberating through the quiet neighborhood as the year began anew. The world outside stood witness to a desperate act, another attempt by a Tadeu, whether the one fighting for survival or the one seeking to end it, lost in the throes of despair.

Trapped in his own misery, each version of Tadeu wrestled with the weight of expectations and failures. They fought to carve out a unique identity in lives that felt so achingly similar. But with each effort, they stumbled, falling into the same patterns, echoing the same mistakes.

As the echoes of the gunshot faded, the street remained silent, a testament to their struggles, two lives intertwined yet so profoundly separate, forever chasing the elusive hope of becoming something more than just another Tadeu lost in the labyrinth of existence. In that moment, both men were reminded that they were bound by their own choices, doomed to repeat the cycle of their failures, and forever haunted by the specter of what could have been.

# Forty-Three

Beto was single again, having finally buckled under Aline's relentless pressure to marry once more. Aline had been furious about the breakup, she truly believed they were going to get married.

Beto, on the other hand, couldn't have cared less. It was astonishing how unaffected he was by other people's problems. His lack of empathy was one of his most defining traits.

Sipping a cup of coffee, he sat at a wooden table on the bustling sidewalk of a café, gazing into the distance, thinking about work as always. That's when he spotted Cintia, with her hair tied back in a ponytail, tray in hand, scanning the area for a place to sit and enjoy her cappuccino and croissant. He raised his arm and waved her over, hoping she would notice him. After a few seconds, he invited her to share the table with him. "You can sit at my table; it's very crowded. You won't find another place," he called out.

"Oh, thank you!" she replied, a hint of relief in her voice as she made her way over. She set the tray down on the table and sat across from Beto.

"How are you? Everything okay?" Beto asked, trying to sound casual. "I'm sorry about what happened between you and Tadeu. I heard you're not together anymore."

He definitely didn't feel sorry about the breakup.

"No need to be sorry. Now I can focus on what really matters," she said, releasing an inviting smile that was both awkward and entirely provocative.

Beto felt his face flush at her words. He hadn't expected *that response.* There was something in her tone, a spark of possibility, that ignited a flicker of hope within him. The dynamics had shifted, and for the first time, he considered that perhaps this was an opportunity.

# Forty-Four

Detective Antunes parked in front of the apartment that Tadeu had rented in the capital city. He was accompanied by two support subordinates, properly dressed and armed. Antunes knocked on the door. No response. After a few minutes, he knocked again.

Finally, a worn-out Tadeu appeared at the door, looking thin, unshaven, disheveled, and clad in pajamas that desperately needed washing.

"You're under arrest for Pedro's death, young man. Come with me to the station. Did you really think threatening the former mayor to remove your name from the investigation would work?"

"I threatened the former mayor? When?"

Before I go, I'd like to leave a simple thank-you:

To my wife, Cristina, who always supports me, even in my craziest ideas.
To my father, Milton, for encouraging my artistic side from the very beginning.
To my mother, Ana, and the fond memories I have of us renting horror movies to watch together.
And to my brother, Tei, the coolest person I've ever known.

9 781998 662876